The Obsessed Hero and the Villainous Family's Daughter

악역가문의 막내딸에게 남주가 집착하면

WRITTEN BY OU HEUNG

EDITIO

PUBLISHING

The Obsessed Hero and the Villainous Family's Daughter

© Ou Heung

Cover Illustration by MUMONG

악역가문의 막내딸에게 남주가 집착하면 by Ou Heung

This English edition was published by Editio Publishing LLC in 2022 by exclusive contract with Kyobo Book Centre Co. Ltd.

ISBN 979-8-9863835-9-0 (Print)

Printed in the United States of America

https://editiopublishing.com/

The Obsessed Hero and the Villainous Family's Daughter

CONTENTS

CHAPTER ONE

Tragedy struck all at once.

I was only twenty-five when I died so suddenly, but just as suddenly, I was reincarnated.

They say death and birth are inseparable, but I didn't think both would happen so close together. It's pointless to go on and on about how I died, how terrible my life had been, how hopelessly destitute I had been in that first life... so let's skip that.

The important part is where I ended up, and what my new life was like. I retained my memories from my previous life throughout my early childhood, and I was pretty pleased with that, at least. In this life, I had a caring mom and dad, an older brother who was always delighted to see me, and two older twin sisters who would carry me around all day. I was coddled and treasured to the point that I hardly ever needed to walk on my own.

Man, what an upgrade from my last life. Everything would be better here. Easier. Happier. I just thought my life was all set, you see.

Then everything came crashing down.

On my seventh birthday, my father announced, "Our Estella is old enough to start taking lessons now."

I was ecstatic. The time had come to take classy private lessons like all the young noble ladies do in movies and novels. I'd get to have teatime like an elegant lady, learn how to arrange colorful flowers, do intricate embroidery, take dance lessons...

But I was way off base. The collection of gifts I received on my birthday made that very clear.

"D-dad?" I managed. "What's all this?"

The gifts filled an entire storage room. The jewels encrusted on each item glinted in the sunlight that shone through a small window, and each gift was so expensive and dazzling that I had to shield my eyes. But they weren't items suitable for a young lady of noble birth.

Instead, all kinds of blades from daggers to longswords, a heavy ball chained to a sickle, javelins, and spears twice my size, a huge bow you'd only see in video games... and what in the world is that thing with the spiky metal ball?

Everything in the storage room was a weapon. I blinked.

"Oh my, does nothing suit your tastes, Estella? Take a good look at this sword. This sword belonged to Count Kiskalla III, and it has bathed in the blood of thousands.

Legend has it..." And so, dad began his endless description of the weapons that were supposed to be a child's birthday gifts.

"S-so all these weapons are legendary?" And they were used to kill thousands?

"That's right, Estella," he beamed down at me. "Aren't they fantastic?"

Unable to reply, my mouth hung open. I needed an explanation as to why an ordinary seven-year-old little lady like myself was getting weapons for her birthday. I preferred playing house, cooking up imaginary soups by mashing up weeds with little rocks, or even playing jacks with pebbles.

"It's just like I told you, dear," my mother explained. "Estella is more interested in concocting poisons. I saw her experimenting with poisonous plants."

"No, mom. That's not what I was doing. Not poisons! I was just playing house!"

"Oh my... is that right, Estella?" my father asked. "I guess I didn't know you well enough. In that case, we'll start building a laboratory for you straight away. You can start with poison-making lessons tomorrow. Wouldn't that be great?"

Wouldn't that be great? Wouldn't that be... dad's question echoed in my head.

"And this armory is yours as well," he kept on. "So, feel free to come here whenever you like. And if you need a sparring partner..." dad's eyes glinted. "Just let me know."

Along with the thought that I should never ask for a sparring partner, I finally realized that I had not just been reincarnated.

I had taken over a character in a novel.

The epiphany hit me like a book over the head. I had become a character *in* a book. More specifically, I was the youngest daughter of a family of villains with absolutely no hope for that bright future I had so hoped for.

House Kartina was a family of irredeemable villains.

The Kartinas, including me—now that I had taken over this life—were not the kind of villains who meddled in silly little wrongdoings. We didn't engage in acts like throwing drinks at people at social gatherings, stealing things to frame someone, or even just accusing the protagonist's family of treason and starting ruinous rumors.

Unfortunately, they were the kind of villains who kidnapped and tortured people for no reason, who then sold them off as slaves to other countries once they got bored, or started wars between countries for fun and profit...

They were like kings of the criminal underworld.

Kind of like the mafia, so to speak. Or the Hong Kong triad? In any case, they were cruel and awful. So cruel to the point that, in my past life, before I had joined this villainous story, I had actually had to stop reading during the most crucial moments in the novel!

Being the worst kind of antagonists, their relationship with the protagonist was also the worst. They killed his parents, sold his sister off to another country as a slave, annihilated every family that helped him, and when it came to the woman he loved...

I'll spare you the details. The Kartinas were villains in a hardcore, R-rated novel aimed at a male audience, so you can imagine the atrocities my new family committed.

"Estella, I caught a monster! Do you want it?"

"Estella, I stole a book full of recipes for poisons from a hundred years ago. It's for you."

"You must be tired from your lessons. Would you like me to buy you a slave masseuse from the Western Empire, Estella?"

But even though they were all villains and psychopaths, every single member of my family loved me dearly. Estella, Estella, Estella... Even in my sleep, I could hear them calling me. Their love for me was fierce and exceptional. Despite all the horror they committed, they not only protected me, but doted on me.

And so, I grew up as the beloved Estella of the Kartina family.

I've lived as a Kartina for seventeen years.

In that time, I've become adept in all kinds of skills villains excel in, such as sword fighting, martial arts, making bombs, shooting poison needles, archery, mind domination, seduction, and a myriad of other nefarious talents mastered only by those in the family.

"Apparently our little Estella failed her poison-making advancement exam."

"We can't just stand idly by. Should I steal the answer key?"

"There's no need for that. I'll beat up the proctor, so don't worry, Estella!"

I smiled awkwardly at my siblings, who were ready to commit all kinds of crimes for me.

House Kartina had a very rigorous education curriculum. You could only be assigned even basic missions and be acknowledged as a proper member of the Kartina family after you achieved the minimum rank. That minimum was the class-two rank in all kinds of subjects, and I'd been sitting just below that rank for years now. My family was terribly worried, but I didn't care. I'd been carefully, deliberately maintaining that rank. If I wanted, I could get to the first rank in every subject and receive the scarlet badge given to only the best students.

"Don't worry, Estella. I've got your back. You won't ever need to face the bad guys." My sister Ayla, who must have thought my awkward face meant I was worried about my future, stroked my hair affectionately.

Ayla, *we* are the bad guys.

"I'm here too, Estella. Your brother will protect you." Kalen patted my shoulder reassuringly.

My brother and sisters seemed anxious about me feeling discouraged. Aww man, don't make me feel bad! But I needed to hide my true proficiency, lest I be thrown into the real villainy, so I kept my mouth shut. I'd keep their misconception of me as fragile and weak—and even encourage it.

"*Pfft!* You? The guy who failed to assassinate Viscount Velot's son not too long ago?" Ada, the short-haired twin sister, spoke up.

I gasped. The tea in the cup I was holding rippled with the tremble of my hand. Stay calm.

"What? Bahaha! You mean the Velot family's son who was just knighted? You couldn't take care of that small fry?" Ayla, whose long hair was twisted up in a bun, laughed at Kalen.

The atmosphere tensed. Kalen, whose pride was apparently wounded, scowled. "That bastard hired an insanely skilled mercenary. He blocked all my shuriken. That's not a normal skill level. The smoke bomb he used was high-quality as well." Kalen's expression darkened. "I'll get that mercenary if it's the last thing I do."

I spat out my tea at his declaration of violence.

"Oh? What's wrong, Estella?" My sister looked over at me, worried.

"Th-that person, the Velot family's son. Is he a bad person? So bad that you have to kill him?" I asked.

"Of course. That thieving bastard caught the deer I was hunting."

Oh... I guess his motive for murder was clear, at least? I was at a loss for words.

"I'll take care of him for you. I'll go to the Velot estate tonight, seduce him and cut his throat!"

"Ada!" Ayla yelled.

At least Ayla was somewhat normal. I hoped that she would stop the other two.

"Estella is listening," Ayla scolded. She covered my ears.

And then the twins whispered over my head. "There's an aphrodisiac in my room that dulls all pain."

Oof. I let out a loud sigh. I guess I won't be able to go to bed early tonight. Again. Because the Velot family's son needed to be rescued before my sisters got to him.

You may have realized by now, but unbeknownst to my family, I have been interfering with my siblings' misdeeds all along.

"I'll take care of the son and find out who that mercenary was," Kalen growled.

"The mercenary? Is that really necessary, Kalen? How would he have blocked your attacks? I'm sure it was a coincidence." I wiggled out of Ayla's grasp as I spoke.

"No, he's unreal. I need to find out who he is and what organization he's from." Kalen's brow furrowed, and he gritted his teeth.

I gulped, lowering my head, and looking at my reflection in my teacup. I tried to breathe. They must never find out. That I, Estella, was that so-called mercenary who saved Viscount Velot's son.

Technically, dealing with any of my siblings individually was no issue, though I might be in trouble if all three of them attacked me at once. I had no idea as to why I was so adept at villainous activities, but the moment I realized at the age of seven that I had been taken over by a character in a novel, all of my potential as Estella was unlocked.

Maybe this body remembered having lived through the plot once before? I was new to this role, but for the original Estella's time had looped, after all. The Estella in the novel may have been a despicable villainess who died at the hands of the protagonist before she could use all her abilities on him, but those abilities were outstanding.

Let me make one thing clear. Estella was not just an antagonist from any old romantic fantasy novel; she could defeat the knights of the empire with her bare hands and destroy a whole troop with just a sword. Estella was one of the leading candidates to become the Kartina family successor.

And me, as this Estella—I hid my abilities. I had been hiding them as best as I could since I came into this world and into this role. I acted like I had none.

Because my family, the Kartinas, would give anyone capable—man, woman, or child—violent criminal missions. I may have been born a Kartina, but I had no desire to willingly partake in the murder and torture of people. Instead, I worked hard to create an image of a tenderhearted girl who was no good at hurting anyone, a girl who liked books—even though they just make me sleepy—who disliked blood, and who envisioned hope in the world.

And I succeeded.

Then one day, I thought to myself, why not something more? What if I took it one step further? What if I went around rectifying all the wrongdoings my family committed? Maybe that would mitigate some of the backlash when House Kartina falls.

So, I saved someone my siblings had tormented for no reason—and boy did it feel great. I didn't dare mess with whatever my parents were doing, but I could at least amend whatever offenses my siblings were committing. I've already saved fifty people so far. Man, I bet I'll go to heaven.

But the nail that sticks out gets hammered down. It's obvious what would happen if my siblings found out I had obstructed their work. What if they attacked me all at once, blinded by rage? I wouldn't be sad if I lost against them, but I didn't want to hurt my brother or sisters. Throughout the seventeen years of my life with them, I had been showered with affection.

It's a shame, but once Viscount Velot's son was safe, I would have to lay low for a while. Now that Kalen was determined to catch this mercenary, it would only be a matter of time until I was caught if I wasn't careful.

But my plans were dashed soon after... thanks to the hero.

CHAPTER TWO

Boom!

Fire erupted when the bomb I threw crashed against the wood of the small stable. Smoke rose high above the billowing flames. The destructive power of the bomb was incredible.

Small, yes, but it sure packed a punch.

I smiled in relief, thinking of the horses that had already safely escaped into the shelter of the forest. Everything had gone according to plan. I knew there would be a bomb-throwing lesson, and I knew the stable was the target. I wanted to prevent senseless killing, so I shooed the horses off before sunrise. All of the horses in the stable were old and sick, and it would be nice for them to spend the rest of their lives roaming free in nature after years of hard work.

"Estella, did that frighten you?"

Like a reflex, I began to tremble. Seeing my reaction, Kalen leaned in, gently wrapping his arm around my shoulders. Above me, his luscious silver hair fluttered in the breeze. He had a beautiful face that you could never forget.

But don't be fooled by his appearance; he was capable of shattering bones into a thousand tiny pieces while wearing a smile on that beautiful face.

I nodded quickly and didn't forget to quake in my pretend fear.

"Estella would never say she was frightened. Don't you get it? Unsophisticated weapons like bombs don't suit Estella. We need to teach her swordsmanship. Just imagine how graceful Estella would be with a sword encrusted with colorful jewels! Come with me, Estella." My older twin sister, Ada, took my hand and dragged me along.

Ada was wrong. I didn't want to learn more about bombs or swords. What do jewels on a sword matter if shedding blood with it? Such a sword will still cause pain. It will still kill. Bomb or sword or whatever else; they are all just means to kill people.

For seventeen years, I have been demonstrating my incompetency at any and all torture and killing techniques, but my siblings refused to give up on me. They were concerned about me carrying the Kartina name without any skills. It was important for both our reputation and survival, as we had many enemies, both within and outside the family.

It was worse when another Kartina was the enemy.

Unlike a typical noble family where the eldest son was expected to inherit everything, our family operated under a system of succession that forced its members to turn against each other. Among our family members, anyone could become the successor. Hence the fierce, often deadly, competition.

Did they use political machinations?

No.

All you needed to do was to obtain a signed statement from the other, conceding their right to succession, using any means possible. The issue being "any" means. My father, Stefan, the current Count Kartina, was the third son of the previous count. He had mutilated his oldest brother Schubert's arm and kidnapped his older brother Schuron's fiancée.

Stefan had managed to become the next family head, but that didn't guarantee that one of his children would become the next successor. The children of Schubert and Schuron had it out for us. Fortunately, Ada, Ayla, Kalen, and I were too close to even consider fighting each other.

"Swordsmanship? You want our little Estella to carry a heavy weapon like that? I will kill you if her cute little hands get blisters! It's better for her to learn more elegant ways like torture."

"Torture isn't elegant, Ayla. I smiled awkwardly as I looked at Ayla and Ada, who each held one of my hands. Can we please stop?"

"Ha... I guess you can't be talked to. Hold your sword, Ayla."

"My sword? Who fights with swords these days?" Ada let go of my hand and procured several vials from her pocket. Her eyes shone malevolently as she placed the vials between her fingers.

This is bad.

As Ada shook her hands, black liquid sloshed inside the vials. I recognized it: a horrifying liquid that melted human flesh upon contact.

"If you're fighting over Estella, don't leave me out." Kalen took a fist-sized bomb out of his pocket.

You too?

I tried not to squeeze my sisters' hands too tightly. Things were escalating. It wasn't just a silly little fight between siblings. It wouldn't stop with some hair getting pulled and faces getting bruised. Our fights were...

I recalled a fight from a few days ago. It was laughable no matter how many times I thought about it, but they had fought over who would get to eat lunch with me. They had fought over nothing. And the outcome?

The east servants' wing was destroyed. Some of the servants were injured. Quite a few of them had such serious injuries—some of them wouldn't be able to work for a while.

With bombs, poisons, and swords, this fight wasn't going to be any different, if not worse. Please, please stop. I didn't want innocent people to get hurt.

I took a deep breath and announced, "I want to learn it all. I'll learn everything so I don't bring shame to the Kartina name!"

All three gazes snapped to the top of my head. It wasn't that I was that short; they were just unnecessarily tall. Their eyes, which had just been burning with fury, quickly softened into expressions of adoration.

My three siblings embraced me at the same time.

"Oh my! Look at our Estella, so eager to learn."

I couldn't be less interested in learning how to kill people, but it was the only thing that could stop this fight.

"What will you study first, Estella? Making bombs, right?"

Damn it.

I had no idea my declaration would spark yet another fight.

In the end, a fight broke out, and the outcome was disastrous. The prized field of poisonous plants belonging to our mother and the lady of the house, Hela Kartina, burned.

"How dare you fight in front of Estella! Are you insane?" Hela Kartina, with her snowy white skin and cherry red lips, was the most villainous of them all. An expert in all poisons in the empire, she had a gift for *enticing* someone to consume any poison no matter what it took.

"We apologize, mother." Kalen and the twins had kneeled in front of our mother.

"Which bone should I break?" Hela glowered down at her children and stretched out her elegant fingers. I flinched with each crack of her knuckles.

The punishments weren't ordinary, either. This was a familiar sight, but I still couldn't get used to it. It was too harsh a punishment for a fight between siblings. Not just harsh. If this had been my previous life in Korea, this moment would have made the news.

I do believe that evil deeds deserve retribution, but if you look at it that way, not a single person in this family would go without severe punishment. As guilty as they were, I had no desire to watch the siblings I'd grown up with these past seventeen years undergo such cruelty.

I blinked rapidly, turning my head to the side, and opening my mouth wide. My eyes filled up with tears because of the forced yawn.

Excellent. Before my tears could dry up, I grabbed the hem of Hela's skirt. "Mom, my siblings, they aren't to blame. It's all my fault. I'm just so incompetent…"

Drip. A single tear trailed down my cheek with perfect timing. I should be an actor.

"Estella, don't blame yourself. It's not your fault." Hela wrapped her arms around me.

I raised my head in Hela's embrace, sniffing dramatically. "Mom, I think I'd be really upset if they got punished." My blue-green eyes met her red ones.

"I see. You're so considerate of your siblings, my little Estella. How are you so different from them?" Hela ran her hand over my curly blonde hair.

"Does that mean you forgive them, mom?"

Hela's gaze wavered. I prayed that she would make a wise decision.

"All right," she conceded. "Since Estella appealed to me so sincerely, I'll forgive you. In exchange, you'll come shopping with me, won't you, Estella?"

"Yes, mom." I beamed, noticing Kalen, Ada, and Ayla sigh in relief out of the corner of my eye. They were blessed with the monstrous physical resilience of the Kartina family, but even they must've wanted to avoid broken bones.

There's something I should mention here. What they worried about was not the physical pain, but rather its potential to hinder their evildoing.

"But you should take responsibility for what you've done, don't you agree?"

"Yes, mother." All three of them replied at once.

This seemed to please Hela, who smirked and assigned them a mission instead of punishing them. "Bring Rodrigo Duveli Erhart here."

"What? Who did you say, mom?" I was so surprised that I had to ask her again.

"Rodrigo Duveli Erhart, the empire's archduke," Hela began, her tone shifting. "What is it, my darling? Are you interested in him?" Her expression quickly turned cold as she spoke.

"N-n-no. Of course not. I don't even know who he is." A lie. I knew very well who he was, and I was very interested in him. Because in the story, it was Rodrigo who would ruin this family! He was the man Estella was in love with and who abhorred her. He was also the hero of the story.

"That's right. You don't need to know him, my darling Estella." Hela, who seemed satisfied with my answer, smiled and hugged me tightly.

My heart began to pound against my chest. Am I going to meet the protagonist after all? Is there no way to avoid him? I've been good for seventeen years. Oh, heartless God. How cold of you. Are you dooming me after all?

"Estella?" Hela asked, catching sight of my gloomy expression. I forced my lips into a smile. "Estella," she said, "if anything worries you, just say so. We are the Kartinas. We have nothing to fear or worry about."

Of course! I'm a Kartina! A Kartina who can make the impossible possible! I will find a way to survive. The Kartina family had a few sayings handed down from previous generations. One of the most relied upon being: "If you don't want to get killed, kill first."

I've been using a slightly modified version of this saying, which goes, "If you don't want to get killed, save lives."

To be perfectly honest, it wouldn't be strange for any one of my relatives to get struck by lightning, considering all the evil things they've done. That's why I wanted to do good. I didn't want to get stabbed in the street or get poison all over me and wither away like dry rice.

I made up my mind: I'll save Rodrigo. If my family members commit nothing but evil, then I, in turn, will do something good for the hero.

A zero-sum game! That was my plan.

"The day of the kidnapping will be in one week, on the day of the ball. Isn't it a perfect occasion? Rodrigo has so many enemies, it won't be easy to figure out who did it."

There was only one reason why Hela had decided on the day of the ball. "It's a perfect day to make a scene."

I could almost sense Hela's heart beginning to pound faster with excitement.

He's in danger. The protagonist is in danger. This is no time to stand by and watch. I have to act.

"Mom, I want to go to the ball too." I begged with twinkling eyes.

"That's..." Hela began to answer.

She just needs to say "fine" now.

"...not possible."

Much to my surprise, however, she refused my request.

CHAPTER THREE

Not the answer I had expected. I was sure that she'd be delighted. I knew I'd need a new dress and jewelry to go to a ball. I could wear something I already owned, but most noblewomen would at least alter a previously worn dress, for example, by changing the ribbons, to give it a fresh look. This did not apply to less affluent families, of course. So, whenever there was a grand ball, queues would form outside popular boutiques and jewelers, and some would even require customers to get numbers for the waiting lists.

In other words, if Estella were to attend the ball, Hela would get to do things she loved, such as shopping with her daughter and intimidating people with how much money she had. So why did she refuse?

"Why, mom?" I prodded further, out of character for me since I normally tried to be as accommodating as possible. Plus, it was taboo for a Kartina to ask a higher-ranking person "why." Asking "why" was equivalent to asking for a fight.

"I'm worried that people will fall for you. It annoys me just to think about all those ugly bastards making advances at you."

Huh? Do you want me to never leave the house?

Hela continued. "The ball is especially bad. What are the purposes of balls and masquerades? Everyone has only one thing in mind, even while laughing elegantly and pretending to have deep conversations. They want to find a catch. Now, imagine you were to attend, Estella. It would be chaos. They'd flock to you like moths to a flame. They don't know their place. You should just live with me forever." Hela was an elegant woman. In terms of her appearance, not her actions. Whenever harsh words escaped those elegant lips, it gave me a little thrill. But not today.

"Oh, mom. I may be showered with affection at home, but that will not be the case elsewhere. You only adore my pitiful self because we're family." I told her as I waved my hands dismissively.

"Estella! What are you saying?!" Kalen burst out. "No one in the empire could rival your beauty. Is that how you've seen yourself all this time? That breaks my heart!"

Hm? Did I say something wrong? For the past twenty-five years, I'd been taught that humility was a virtue. In my past life, that is. What I had just said was an automatic response.

I knew I was pretty, but that didn't mean that I was able to go around bragging about it.

"Mother, we've got to do something. Our dear Estella seems to be unaware of how beautiful she is. I will personally gouge out the eyes of every bastard who ogles her, so please allow her to come with us."

I didn't quite understand what had angered Kalen, but things were going in my favor.

"Ha…" Hela was faced with a dilemma.

"I'll stick close to my siblings." I promised, urging Hela to make the right decision. Her brows furrowed. I stared at her pleadingly as she weighed her options in silence.

Finally, her face softened. "All right," she said. "I suppose our dear Estella needs a chance to view herself objectively." She smiled brightly at us, and I breathed in a sigh of relief. "Now," Hela continued, "shall we go shopping?"

Plop.

I collapsed onto my bed as soon as we returned to the mansion, having realized yet again that shopping was more exhausting than most types of training.

"Was it tiring, my lady?" Jane spoke up knowingly as she noticed the many new boxes the other servants carried into the room.

Jane, my personal maid, had a physique similar to mine, as well as hair of similar length and color. Though my hair was a bright blonde and hers was more of a dirty blond. She served as my body double in emergencies.

"Jane... I'm so tired." I whined out the word and acted like a child. Jane just clicked her tongue.

Anyone could tell we didn't have a relationship like most ladies and their maids. I treated Jane like a friend. It was hard not to, seeing that we were the same age and had grown up together. She was the only person I could pour my heart out to.

I also felt indebted to Jane, who had taken a blood oath to sacrifice herself to save me in an emergency, so it was hard to even think about ordering her around like a common servant.

"Are you really going to the ball, my lady?" Jane was taken aback by the pile of boxes stacked along one of the walls of my room, which was the size of a training hall in any ordinary nobleman's mansion. Putting aside the task of opening the boxes, she approached my bed.

"Why? Are you worried that I'll be bothered by all the men flocking to me?"

"Huh?" Jane made a strange grimace with her upper lip raised and her eyes narrowed. "Does it look like I'm worried about you?"

"You're not?"

Jane shook her head to dismiss the thought.

"Then who are you worried about?"

"The guys." Jane stretched out her hand and drew a circle with her finger as if to trace the men she imagined buzzing around the ball like flies. She said, "When I'm retired and ready to get married, there has to be at least one fly left for me. But if you go to the ball, every man there will look at you, whether they fall for you or not. Their eyes could meet yours by accident. Good lord! May God have mercy."

Jane clasped her hands together in an exaggerated prayer motion, then continued. "Do you think the young master and the young mistresses will let them be? Of course not."

I gulped. Jane pretended to draw her hand across her neck.

The Kartinas were known to be reckless, but Jane *had* to be exaggerating. As if they would kill anyone just for meeting my gaze.

I threw a pillow at Jane in response to her silly comment, but she avoided it easily and laughed.

"The sun has gone down, my lady." Jane pointed to the window. Just as she said, the sun had disappeared behind the mountains.

I shot up from the bed. Amidst all the chitter chatter, I had completely forgotten...

"Don't stay out too late," Jane said, handing me the black clothes and sword that had been hidden in the closet.

It was time to rescue Viscount Velot's son.

Rescuing Viscount Velot's son was an easy task. He just needed to be surrounded by people.

That night, I threw heavy rocks at his mansion and shattered all the windows. Naturally, the Velot household erupted into chaos. They thought a thief had broken into the mansion, and soon the city guard arrived.

I let out a sigh of relief. With the guards here as well, even a Kartina wouldn't try and kill someone. It wasn't worth the risk.

"I'm tired."

Why couldn't I have been transported into an ordinary romance novel? I gnashed my teeth and flipped off whichever god had sent me here before heading back to the warmth of my bed.

A week later, it was the day of the ball.

"You look beautiful." Jane's simple compliment was sincere. She was a very helpful maid who would give me a reality check whenever I was in danger of losing touch thanks to my overly affectionate and doting family.

Jane rarely complimented me and was incapable of flattery, so hearing a compliment from her gave me a confidence boost. My apparently pleasant appearance was confirmed by Stefan, who stood in the doorway dabbing his eyes with a handkerchief.

I really am pretty. I looked at my reflection in the mirror one last time. I had Hela's blonde hair. My golden hair, meticulously maintained with money earned through wrongdoings, had a lustrous sheen no matter which way I turned. My skin was ivory white, and my large round eyes, sharp nose, and red lips were angelic.

I was a classic beauty, and the cherry on top was the beauty mark under my right eye, which crinkled when I smiled. I took after my parents' best qualities and was even prettier than my sisters, who were known to be quite beautiful.

This wasn't me being delusional. It was a fact written in the novel.

"Estella, it's not too late to change your mind. Why don't you go to a ball where I can go with you? No, I'll hold a ball just for you," Stefan told me as he approached.

He was lying. There was something I found out while preparing for this ball. I'm seventeen years old, and I will be an adult next year. In the Philemon Empire, one could debut into society up to two years before coming of age. Wealthy and powerful families sent their daughters to their debutante balls as soon as they turned sixteen, not wasting any time. Their intent was to have them enter high society as soon as possible to secure good husbands.

And though I was a wealthy and powerful Kartina, I still hadn't debuted, even at the age of seventeen. The reason was simple.

Stefan had prevented my high society debut, openly stating that "Estella doesn't need to marry." This was in contrast to my sisters, who had gotten their extravagant debutante balls as soon as they had turned sixteen.

"I'll see you when I come home," I told Stefan.

In other words, today's ball was going to be my official debut into high society.

There wasn't much to debutante balls; they were simply events at which a young noble lady made her first appearance in high society. The more powerful the host, the better the occasion for debutantes. This didn't matter much in my case. I was a Kartina. Even if my debutante ball had been held in a shabby barn, I would be hard to ignore.

I got on my tiptoes and kissed Stefan on both cheeks. If I delayed any further, he might have knocked me out to keep me from going.

Stefan smelled like a particular drug that could knock someone out immediately.

As I tried to quickly distance myself from him, Stefan urgently called out to me. "Estella, wait."

Stefan pulled out a few colorful feather ornaments from his pocket, and he carefully placed a few of them in my hair.

"Dad..." I murmured. I was thankful to Stefan, who had brought me a gift even though he didn't want me to go. His fond gaze remained on my face for a long while.

After a few moments of peaceful silence, Stefan broke the spell of quiet. "Estella," he said, "the tips of these feathers are soaked in poison. If any ugly bastards come at you, just stab them. I'll take care of the rest."

I thought it was weird when he placed feathers in my hair, but there was more to it than mere decoration. I smiled awkwardly. "Thank you, dad."

Time to get on the carriage.

Hela had some business to take care of in the countryside, so she wasn't home. Stefan also had places to be, so he didn't delay me any longer. My siblings got on their horses. I was the only occupant of the heavy-laden carriage. The carriage was just filled with weapons. As the carriage rumbled forward, I took a few deep breaths. It was finally time to meet Rodrigo, the male lead of the story.

I'll save you.

Just save me in exchange.

I clenched my fists.

CHAPTER FOUR

Rattle!

There's nothing comfortable about riding a carriage. In other words... *It sucks.*

The Kartina carriage was made by the empire's foremost carriage maker. Everything, from the wheels to the smallest decorations, was expensive. Still, riding in it was so uncomfortable due to the recent rain that had left the roads uneven.

The roads should have been fixed, but all government employees of the empire were lazy, without exception. *It's so problematic.* I shook my head.

Whenever the carriage drove over a bump in the road, my body was tossed up and down. I missed the fresh air and having my feet on the ground. I really want to get off...

Judging by the line of carriages outside the window, which was cracked open slightly, it was going to take a while.

"Estella, how are you?" Ada opened the window and asked me.

"Can you stay in the carriage a little longer?"

Kalen, Ayla, and Ada rode horseback beside the carriage as if guarding me, even though they could have gone ahead.

"I'm a little tired," I told them, but it's all right." It's not like there's any other way… or is there?

In novels like this, there are scenes where a line of carriages splits apart like the red sea to make way for a wealthy and influential family.

"I'm actually a bit ti—"

"Just say the word. There are bombs under your seat." Kalen announced, smiling brightly as he stuck his head through the window.

I quickly composed myself and sat up straight. "I'm not tired."

Seriously, the Kartinas are unbelievable. They thought of blowing up the other carriages first instead of using their influence to move the carriages. *Oh God, once again I have saved the lives of dozens of people.* Before Kalen could keep asking, I hurriedly closed the window.

Time passed by uneventfully inside the carriage. Staring at floating dust particles, I thought about the countless people who had died in the story. *Will I be able to recognize Rodrigo?* I wondered.

Then I let out a short laugh. *There's no way I wouldn't.* He was the male lead, so he was bound to be gorgeous. Or have some kind of halo behind him. But just in case, I tried to remember everything I could about Rodrigo.

It wasn't hard to remember him, probably because he was the person I was fated to fall in love with.

Rodrigo Duveli Erhart. The empire's archduke. A rare master swordsman, he managed to produce an aura around his sword at the age of five and went to fight his first battle at ten. He started out as a regular soldier and quickly rose through the ranks after distinguishing himself in war. It was at the age of twelve that he became the leader of a knight order consisting of a hundred knights.

After that, every battle he participated in resulted in victory, and, at the age of fifteen he earned the title of "Myriad Sergeant" given only to those who had killed ten thousand enemy soldiers. So, was sword fighting all he was good at?

No, that was just a given. Just as it was a given for the male lead in a romance novel to be wealthy, good swordsmanship was a basic requirement. He was resourceful as well, and obviously one of the most good-looking men on the continent.

According to the story's description of him, he was a man with dangerous charm. He even knew how to use magic, though only a little. In other words, he was OP, an overpowered character. But that was the seed of misfortune for Rodrigo—because Emperor Thereo wanted to keep him in check.

Thereo was a snake. There was no end to his greed, and he was endlessly malicious. While the Kartinas enjoyed evildoing, the act of transgressing itself, Thereo capitalized on our family's nature to make a profit. He used anyone and everything and simply discarded them when they were no longer useful.

That was Thereo's principle. Just as chocolate and feces are similar in color, but entirely different, the Kartinas and Thereo were worlds apart. He would do anything for money, power, and women.

It's a bit awkward to say this since it sounds biased, but if the Kartinas were like chocolate, Thereo was like feces. If there was anything human about him, it was that Thereo very much adored his son, the Crown Prince, Detheus.

Emperor Thereo tormented Rodrigo to keep the throne stable for Detheus' sake. Rodrigo wasn't aware of this yet, but it was Emperor Thereo who had led Rodrigo's parents to their deaths and had sent him to war at such a young age, saying that his talent was indispensable.

And whenever Rodrigo found someone to care for, the emperor would use the Kartinas or some other sinister force to eliminate them.

Rodrigo seemed fine on the outside, but his heart had been blackened. The reason this novel gained so many female fans, despite being a hard-core novel aimed at male readers, was thanks to their empathy for Rodrigo's sad past.

Still, Rodrigo suppressed his anger. Even though Emperor Thereo had used the Kartinas and other families to push him to the edge, he had survived, so he forgave them.

It was Estella who was the problem. She fell in love with Rodrigo the moment she saw him at the crown princess' birthday celebration, and, as you by now know, gaining the affection of a Kartina was dangerous. They tended to madly obsess over their objects of desire and crave their attention.

Estella had been the same in the story. With Rodrigo refusing to accept her affections, she slowly began to go mad. In the end, she ended up killing the female lead of the story, the woman he loved. And Rodrigo went berserk.

That marked the beginning of the atrocities that earned the novel its "R" rating. I had no desire to remember my cruel fate. Technically, there was nothing to remember. It had been so violent that I skipped that part.

And that was how the world ended. I wasn't sure if the end of the world being triggered by a few families fighting each other was poor writing or a reflection of how powerful those families were.

The story ended with a description of Rodrigo, smiling as he stood alone atop the bodies of his enemies: the Kartinas, the imperial family, and all the others who had ever wronged him.

My body must have been in that pile too, right?

I had no interest in taking part in such a tragic ending. I had no desire to die or to kill. *So, Archduke Rodrigo, I thought, let's get along.*

Hardening my resolve, I nodded, my lips curling up into a smirk.

"On behalf of Count Kartina… Sir Kalen, Lady Ada, Lady Ayla, and Lady Estella."

The noisy banquet hall suddenly fell silent. Eyes widened and mouths drooped open at the appearance of all four Kartina siblings.

And at a banquet held by Duke Gloria! Duke Gloria had a deep connection with Rodrigo's family. He was one of the few sane characters in the story and a supporter of Rodrigo.

Considering the hostility between the Erharts and the Kartinas, it was only natural for everyone to be shocked by the Kartina siblings making an appearance. Though it was all hushed up, most nobles were aware that the imperial family had used the Kartinas to keep the Erharts in check for generations.

Everyone shot glances at us. Kalen, Ada, and Ayla were used to being stared at and did not pay it any mind, but that wasn't the case for me. I shifted uncomfortably with all the attention, finding myself unable to tell friend from foe.

"May the Goddess bless you. Your journey here must have been troublesome, Sir Kalen." The host and Rodrigo's supporter, Duke Gloria, held out his wrinkled hand as he spoke.

"May the Goddess' light shine on you. It wasn't troublesome at all, Duke Gloria." Kalen politely took Duke Gloria's hand and shook it.

"And who might this be?" After greeting Ada and Ayla as well, Duke Gloria's gaze fixed on me.

I grasped the hem of my light green dress and curtsied. "It is an honor to meet you. My name is Estella. I am the youngest Kartina."

My introduction was elegant. Watching my flawless grace, the people surrounding us gasped.

"Oh, *the* Estella!" Duke Gloria's voice boomed, capturing everyone's attention.

Unlike when our entrance had been announced, this time everyone stared openly at me. A brief moment of silence passed as they ogled, but then whispers erupted all around us.

"Ah..."

"She's pretty. No wonder they say the Kartinas cherish her."

"So, the rumors I heard recently were true."

"What rumors?"

"That the youngest Kartina would be making her debut soon, and that you should avoid eye contact with her at all costs."

"Oh my, why is that?"

"Well, you see..."

The words that followed didn't suit the noblewomen. Such cruel words that did not suit their otherwise elegant mannerisms. I was willing to bet my entire fortune that Count Kartina had fabricated those rumors himself.

I had exceptionally good ears. It wasn't because I was special, but because it was written in the story. It was written that the Kartinas had particularly well-developed physical skills.

This particular trait had its upsides and downsides. I had to listen to things I'd rather not hear sometimes.

And whenever that happened...

"People are being noisy. Do you want me to silence them, Estella?" Kalen quietly whispered in my ear.

"Kalen, I don't want to see blood."

Long ago, when I was very little, there had been a servant girl who had spoken ill of me, and he had taken her tongue and... *Ahem.* That day, I had collapsed in shock and caused quite a stir.

I stopped thinking about it.

Kalen flinched, as if he had considered doing the same kind of thing.

"I must send Count Kartina a thank you gift for sending all of you to grace my banquet with your presence." Duke Gloria said, looking genuinely pleased.

The success of an event like this depended on the status of the guests who attended.

We, the Kartinas, may not have had the most prestigious title, but we were the lords of the underworld. And my family was shrouded in mystery since we rarely attended social events.

Considering this, it was fortunate for the duke to have the Kartinas appear, and even more fortunate for his banquet to be chosen as the venue for their precious youngest daughter's debut.

"Our father will be very pleased," Kalen replied.

Duke Gloria attempted to make conversation, but Kalen gave short answers and openly displayed his discomfort.

Duke Gloria could take a hint. He told us to enjoy the banquet, and then left us. Kalen and Ada also disappeared into the crowd, pretending to socialize, so I was left with Ayla, and I knew I would soon be alone.

"Don't speak with anybody. We'll be back soon," she said. "You wanted to come to an event like this, right? Don't dance with anyone and just enjoy it, all right?" Ayla badgered me as she pinched my cheeks.

"...Yes," I answered hesitantly, my lips all askew.

Ayla gave me a tight hug, going on and on about how cute I looked with my cheeks pinched, how I kept getting cuter as I aged, how it was a mystery as to how adorable I was considering the other Kartinas, and so on.

"Estella," she said, "there are people here as dangerous as wild bears. You have to be careful."

Coming from someone who could rip apart a bear with their bare hands. I bit the inside of my cheek to stop myself from laughing.

"Don't worry, Ayla." I lied, attempting to set her mind at ease.

Ayla might soon collapse out of shock.

Anyway, where is Rodrigo?

CHAPTER FIVE

As soon as I was left alone, some men approached me. For the sake of their lives, I slipped away and avoided them—looking for Rodrigo all the while.

The banquet hall was quite large and bursting with people, but I was able to find him very quickly. He had black hair and red eyes, was taller than most people, and had a solid build. In other words, he was very handsome. The worries I had in the carriage about not being able to find him went out the window. Rodrigo was far too noticeable.

That's definitely him! I hurried toward him, making sure to behave naturally. But then, someone started talking to me. "Lady Estella, could we talk for a moment?"

How foolish. There are always people like this... acting like moths to a flame, not knowing or caring about the consequences. I wanted to ignore him, but I turned and greeted him, glancing at the crest adorning his sleeve.

Oh... The two-headed dog embroidered on the man's sleeve was hard to miss. He was from another villainous family, slightly less prestigious than the Kartinas. This meant that they were inferior in skill and wealth, not that they were any less evil.

The Frey family. No wonder he was brave enough to talk to me. He must have thought that he was fully capable of taking on a few assassins on his own.

"Greetings, Lady Estella," he said. "I am Barbati, the eldest son of the Frey family."

I merely nodded again instead of extending a proper greeting.

"If you don't mind, could I have this first dance?" He held out his hand. Over his shoulder, I could see Ayla smiling seductively at Rodrigo as she approached him.

I wanted to get rid of Barbati as fast as possible. *I mind very much, thank you,* I thought. Instead, I said, "Sorry, I'm quite busy at the moment." Then I scurried over to Rodrigo.

Barbati stretched out his arm to try and grab me, but I was too quick for him. "Wait, Lady Estella!" He was following me. I was in too much of a hurry to care, so I ran.

Ayla opened her mouth to call out to Rodrigo.

"Hello!" Before Ayla could get his attention, I reached Rodrigo just in time. Ayla was behind me, Rodrigo in front.

I could sense Ayla flinch in surprise behind me. *I'll explain later, Ayla.* After taking a deep breath, I lifted my head to look at Rodrigo. Our eyes met. "Hello, Sir Rodrigo."

Rodrigo's eyes were sharp with suspicion, as if he had discovered an intruder.

"I'm Estella Kartina," I introduced myself.

Rodrigo's expression changed at my words. His eyes shone like jewels, as if delighted at finding a new toy to play with. His gaze shifted to Ayla, behind me. As he looked back down at me, Rodrigo's lips curled into a charming smile. Overall, his demeanor seemed temperamental and irritated, but that smile was strangely beautiful. A smile that made my stomach flutter, and heat spread through my body.

"Oh yes, of the Kartinas... I've heard." It was unclear whether he meant that he had heard of me or my family. His well-defined and sleek features came nearer, cold eyes crinkled in a chilling, gorgeous smile. "Is there something you need from me?" His gaze seemed to say, *"It's not like we are on good enough terms for pleasant chit-chat."*

Indeed, there's something I need from you. I returned his smile and held out my hand. "Shall we dance?"

"Is there something you need from me?"

Rodrigo stared down at Estella. He knew he would get mixed up with the Kartinas at this banquet as soon as they had made their entrance. There was no way the Kartinas were attending Duke Gloria's banquet for no reason. They never go anywhere without an objective. Their objective was obvious.

A target. It wasn't hard to figure out that *he* was that target. He knew very well that the Kartinas were targeting Erhart. It was hard to miss their machinations.

The Kartinas even messed with the Erharts' business ventures. For example, it hadn't been long since they had blown up his mines that had previously operated without problem. Many had died in the explosion—which, for the Kartinas, was barely more than a prank.

Convinced that the Kartinas were behind it, Rodrigo had reported this to the emperor, but the emperor dismissed it, citing a lack of evidence, and offered Rodrigo his half-hearted condolences.

Incidents like this had happened a few times. It was only natural that Rodrigo didn't like the Kartinas, and he had done his best to avoid them.

But then, the Kartinas had made an appearance at an event hosted by Duke Gloria, known to be a supporter of Rodrigo. There was no way for him to avoid them. Again, their intentions were obvious. He was sure he would have to at least cross swords with them tonight. It might even result in bloodshed.

But then Estella, the youngest daughter of the Kartinas, stepped in front of him and asked something absurd.

"Shall we dance?"

Is she trying to toy with me? Rodrigo furrowed his brows. The atmosphere turned cold. Rodrigo had always had a frigid disposition, so much so that even his nanny, who had known him for years, would get chills when she saw him sitting with a blank look on his face.

And when he frowned, she would say, "You look like the grim reaper."

Whenever he frowned, people ducked out of his way or even fled. But Estella just smiled serenely at him with her wide puppy-dog eyes and stretched out her hand even further.

A hand clad in a pristine white glove.

That untainted little hand did not suit the blackened Kartinas. She wasn't asking for a fight or handing him a poisoned wine glass but asking for a dance. On top of that, this was her debut into high society. Did she not know the significance of her first dance?

"You, you don't dance?" Estella asked carefully, as Rodrigo continued to stare at her hand.

Carefully? This manner, this approach did not suit the Kartinas. Actually, Estella didn't seem like a Kartina at all. Her eyes were free of malice, her expression innocent, her gaze pure.

He was intrigued. *Is this a new assassination technique? What is she up to?*

Rodrigo took Estella's hand and tugged. He pulled her toward him, wrapping an arm around her slender waist.

"Gah!" Ayla, apparently appalled, gasped as Rodrigo led her sister away.

Kalen and Ada, hiding upstairs to ambush Rodrigo, were also shocked.

Estella could sense how shaken they were. She quickly figured out where each of them was.

"Are you a good dancer? I never had the chance to learn it properly because I was on the battlefield," Rodrigo told her.

"Let me lead," Estella said. She had intended to lead whether or not he was a good dancer. Because somewhere upstairs, Kalen and Ada were waiting for an opportunity to target Rodrigo.

Estella put her hand on Rodrigo's shoulder.

Even though my hand rested on his jacket, I could feel the hardships of his life through my palm. His untamed ferocity and his strong, unshakable physique were not something you could simply hide under a jacket. Embraced by Rodrigo's muscled arms, I raised my heels. *He's huge.* I made an entirely objective observation.

Over his shoulders, my eyes met those of Ayla, whose soul seemed to have left her body. She silently mouthed a question. *"Estella, what are you doing?"*

I mouthed the answer I had prepared. *"Ayla, I'm seducing him!"*

But I was in the middle of dancing, and so distracted by Ayla that I accidentally stepped on Rodrigo's foot.

"I thought you were a good dancer?" His marvelous voice tickled my ears.

"I'm sorry! I was looking somewhere else..."

"Where? Did you hide something upstairs?"

A cold shock rippled through me when he pointed out the second floor. *Did he find out about Kalen and Ada hiding upstairs?* I studied Rodrigo's face.

"Of course not," I replied slyly, quickly waving my hand behind his back.

Go somewhere else, Ayla, I wished at her. My sister glared at the back of Rodrigo's head before disappearing into the shadows. *Phew, now I can concentrate on our conversation.*

"I'll show you my dancing skills now," I told him. "You might not be able to keep up."

"How hard could it be?" Rodrigo smirked, confident.

I smiled awkwardly. *The dance we're about to do isn't so simple.* I was sure he would change his mind soon. The fast-paced dance was not easy to keep up with for someone who hadn't learned how to dance. But, of course, Rodrigo was the male lead. Even though he said he never practiced, he was a very skilled dancer. *I guess the male lead really is good at everything.*

I fixed my gaze on Rodrigo's chin and tensed up. Not too far away, Ada and Kalen waited like predatory cats. They watched us, just waiting for an opening—to shoot poisoned needles at Rodrigo to knock him out.

They were going to shoot before the end of this dance. I would have to protect him without raising suspicions and still continue to dance.

The tempo increased. I wouldn't let them pounce.

The song hurried on and on, and the moment it reached its climax, a silver needle gleamed in the light of the chandelier. The Kartina needles were as thin as a spider web and required flawless precision to use.

And they were almost impossible to detect.

Unless you had seen and touched these weapons before and knew the attack was coming, there was no way to block it. But I was Estella Kartina. I could do it... with just a bit of concentration.

I clenched my right hand on Rodrigo's shoulder. At the unexpected force of my grip, he flinched and turned. As if it were part of the dance, Rodrigo and I twirled to the right, embracing each other.

At the same time, I kicked the inside of my dress. The skirt billowed up and completely covered Rodrigo's thighs. A silver needle embedded itself into the billowing fabric.

Okay, one down.

The poisoned needle was definitely shot by Kalen.

One, two, three.

I blocked exactly three poisoned needle attacks by the time the first dance ended. I felt a bit guilty, thinking about Kalen getting chewed out by Ada right about now. They would never even imagine that I had blocked, or was even able to block, their attacks, so the failure had to be blamed on Kalen's lack of skills.

"That was nice." As soon as the dance was over, Rodrigo stepped away.

"How about another?" I prompted. I hadn't been able to talk with him yet. I held Rodrigo as he tried to step away.

Rodrigo's lips tightened into a harsh line. I knew how laughable I must have looked, like some obsessive woman who had fallen in love with him at first sight.

As expected of the male lead, there were a lot of women in Rodrigo's life. He must have had so many women come up to talk to him and ask for a dance.

It must be tiring, I thought, understanding his displeasure. A beautiful face even a god would envy, a well-trained body, and a severe expression paired with a strangely seductive gaze. No person could resist his charm. *So why couldn't you charm the emperor and the Kartinas!*

"Look here, Lady Estella."

Silence enveloped us. Rodrigo's scarlet eyes rested on me for a while. Then he slowly opened his mouth.

CHAPTER SIX

He took a step toward me, his eyes now as cold as ice, in stark contrast to when we were dancing together. My heart stung. *Could it be because I was in love with him in the story?*

"I hate the Kartinas."

I knew as much, and it was only natural, but it wasn't nice to hear. Trying my best to hide my emotions, I nodded. "That's all right," I said with a kind smile, placing my hand on his arm. "Because I don't hate the Erharts."

He flinched and backed away.

But I did not let him get any further away from me. "Let's talk for a moment."

"I have nothing to say to you," he said. "I believe I have fulfilled my obligations to your debut with that first dance."

No wonder he had agreed to dance with me so quickly. *He was just being a gentleman.* I once again realized that Rodrigo had been a good man before he went berserk. The Kartinas had turned this man into a devil. Estella in the story, to be exact.

"It's not enough." I smiled so that my eyes crinkled, a signature move often used by the Kartinas. But unfortunately, it seemed to only work on the other Kartinas.

Rodrigo's face crumpled into a strange frown, and I frowned inwardly along with him. They said you couldn't spit at a smiling face, but I guess they were wrong.

Left with no other options, I grabbed Rodrigo's arm. Rodrigo, who seemed annoyed, raised an eyebrow, but didn't shake me off. *What a gentleman.*

"The balcony would be best, don't you think?" A rhetorical question. I didn't expect Rodrigo to just go along with whatever I said, so I had to use force. I retrieved the dagger from my sleeve.

Realizing something was wrong, he tried to quickly turn away from me, but I stepped even closer to him. And then I pressed the tip of my dagger against his side.

"There are too many people watching, and this is a banquet hosted by your dear friend, Duke Gloria. If you don't want to make a scene, it would be best to follow me." I whispered hastily, twisting my body so that Ayla, who had been circling us, could see my dagger.

Ayla understood I was in control, so she backed off and watched us from afar.

"Do you really want this to end in bloodshed?" It was a threat. Though I wasn't sure it would work on Rodrigo.

His frigid eyes glared at me.

A chill went up my spine at the look he gave me, and I almost confessed that this was all just for show right then and there. I might have done so anyway... if he hadn't suddenly burst out laughing.

"Hahaha! Lady Estella, you're really..." He laughed like a madman, even with a dagger pointed at his side.

My pride was a little bruised. *Do you know how many things I could do with this dagger? I can do all sorts of things.*

"You're very entertaining. Did you think you could threaten me with such a small dagger?" Rodrigo grabbed my waist and pulled me closer. His large hand covered mine against the dagger.

I waited.

Rodrigo twisted my hand so that the dagger pointed at me. The tip of it pressed against my side now. *Is he going to kill me?* My heart skipped a beat.

He whispered, "If I push just a little bit," *I could feel the blade easing closer as he spoke,* "I can easily tear your dress." Rodrigo's hand brushed down my back. "And stab you through it." Chills prickled my skin. He finished, "How much force do you think I need to exert to rend the flesh of a woman not wearing any armor?"

He wasn't simply caressing me. He was making sure I wasn't wearing some sort of thin mithril chainmail under my dress. As soon as I had pulled out my dagger, Rodrigo's courteous guise had dropped. He must have figured that he didn't owe me any courtesy when I was threatening him.

"Enough force to crush an apple, maybe?" I replied without batting an eye.

Rodrigo narrowed his eyes.

I smiled gently and grabbed his wrist. I didn't turn the dagger toward him. Instead, I pulled his wrist closer to my side.

Rodrigo's face froze. He clenched his hand harder around mine to keep the dagger from stabbing me. *He really is a gentleman.*

There was a short struggle. To anyone else, we were a bit too close and friendly for a man and a woman who had just met. A small sigh escaped his lips.

He must not have expected me to react this way. His expression tensed and then drooped with exhaustion.

"We should talk," I said. Keeping hold of his wrist even as he tried to pull away, I glanced over at the balcony.

"All right, fine," he conceded. "Let's hear what you have to say."

We hurried to the balcony. Rodrigo leaned against the railing, his arms crossed. I closed the doors and drew the curtains to make sure no one could overhear us, but as I did, I locked eyes with Ayla for a moment. Her gaze wavered, worried, and my eyes welled a little.

Ayla clenched her fists and turned toward the banquet hall doors as I finished closing the curtains. I lost sight of her.

Then I heard quiet footsteps on the roof.

I could easily tell that it was the sound of Kalen and Ada moving to the roof from the second floor. *But where did Ayla go?* I started to get impatient. Dealing with all three of my siblings while protecting Rodrigo was nearly impossible. I went straight to the point.

"The Kartinas are after you."

Rodrigo seemed unimpressed with this serious news. "That's nothing new. Are those people up there Kartinas as well?"

Rodrigo asked this as he leaned back against the railing, looking up at the roof. His face was exposed to them.

I paled. "Rodrigo!"

Kalen wouldn't miss a chance like this. As I expected, I heard movement. I threw myself at Rodrigo, wrapped my arms around his neck and clung to him. At the same time, I kicked the railing with both feet.

With the force of the recoil and my body weight, Rodrigo's strong body tipped toward me. And then... *Thunk!* The sound of a heavy weapon embedding itself into the ground.

"Do you have a death wish?" I chided him, trying to keep my voice down.

For a moment, confusion crossed Rodrigo's face. "Of course not." He paused for a moment before continuing. "How long are you going to cling to me?" He looked down.

My thighs were wrapped around his waist. I hadn't moved since dragging him away from the railing, clinging to him like a koala.

"We may have danced together, but this seems a bit too forward for people who just met." His casual tone made heat rise to my cheeks. I frowned and lightly stepped back onto the ground.

Rodrigo's hands, which had been hovering behind my back, fell to his side in an exaggerated motion. "This makes it evident that the Kartinas are after me."

That's what I've been saying! I can't believe it took an obvious assassination attempt for him to believe me.

Rodrigo's eyes darkened. The corners of his lips rose.

I could sense danger emanating from him as he stepped closer to me. It was a completely different attitude from before. My shoulders felt heavier under his gaze, which seemed to make the air itself denser.

"What do you want?" His deep voice seemed to reverberate all the way down to the soles of my feet.

"What are you trying to do to me?"

A regular person would have been frightened at this point. He was intimidating enough to make most people tremble in fear, unable to reply. But I...

"I told you... I am Estella of the Kartina family." I smiled brightly as I answered. "And I'm the person who will save your life."

I grasped his cravat with both hands and pulled him down toward me. He hadn't seen this coming, so Rodrigo let himself be pulled down, and the distance between us was nearly gone. We were close enough for our breaths to intermingle, his oddly sweet.

"What are you—" Before he could finish his sentence, an arrow whistled past where his head had just been. Rodrigo looked at the vibrating arrow stuck in the balcony curtains and at me, still holding onto his cravat.

"I saved you again, just now," I said. Seeing his eyes widen and his gaze quiver made me feel a little better.

"Hah?" He let out a huff of disbelief.

Of course, it would be hard to believe that a Kartina would help him. He was probably thinking that this couldn't be true and that it was a trap. Maybe he thought I was trying to lull him into a false sense of security by pretending to help him, before throwing him into an even deeper pit of despair.

"I understand if you don't trust me," I admitted. "You might think I'm planning something much worse by pretending to help you." It might have been because he was so close, but I could very clearly sense Rodrigo's agitation.

"But think about it," I continued. "I'm a Kartina. We set the whole forest on fire rather than setting a trap to catch a single deer. There's no need to doubt me. I wouldn't waste my time laying out a trap for you."

I knew my words weren't very convincing, but Rodrigo had to believe me if he considered the way the Kartina family had always operated.

"That's right. You're a Kartina." He seemed to believe me. "Why are you trying to save me?"

His suspicion was only natural.

"Who said I was doing this for free? You owe me a favor." If my plan succeeded, my intention was to deliver Rodrigo to his beloved and retreat to a small island somewhere with my family. Then I would pray that the world wouldn't end until I died of old age.

But for that to come true, Rodrigo had to find happiness. He needed to stop hating the Kartinas. He needed to abandon the ill-fated relationships of his past. I was ready to give my all for Rodrigo's happiness. I hoped that, in return, Rodrigo would show me some mercy so that I could find my own happiness.

I had also attempted to rehabilitate the Kartinas. Making it look like a coincidence, I had made my family members meet priests, surreptitiously strewn books on social justice on the floor for them to come across, and even made them attend a charity event... but none of worked.

They had seduced the once-sober priests into drinking alcohol, paid off the authors of those books to corrupt them, and stole everything from the charity event.

There was no way to rehabilitate the Kartinas.

So, Rodrigo was my last hope. Getting on his good side or protecting him from the Kartinas was the only way.

"You may not believe me, but I really do not want you to die." I took a deep breath and placed my hand on his cheek.

His gaze met my blue-green eyes. Even the most talented actor couldn't lie with their eyes. *Please believe me.* "I just want you to be happy."

He froze.

Did my sincerity get through to him?

CHAPTER SEVEN

Ayla bit her nails, almost losing her mind when she saw Estella step out onto the balcony with that wicked bastard. And when Estella closed the curtains, as if telling her not to follow, Ayla nearly went insane. *What if something happens to my dear Estella?*

It was hard to concentrate on the plan when worry wracked her whole body. In the end, she snuck outside to see what was going on—and found them in a compromising position.

That bastard was practically glued to Estella!

Ayla's blood boiled. She couldn't hold back her fury. She grabbed an arrow and let it loose.

But Rodrigo, who seemed to have eyes on the back of his head, managed to dodge the arrow and proceeded to press his body even closer to Estella! Her sister, her innocent little bunny of a sister, had been cornered not just by a wild animal, but a tiger.

Ayla tensed her leg muscles, ready to jump onto the balcony to rescue her, but Estella remained out of reach in

Rodrigo's clutches. She hated Rodrigo but had to admit that he was skilled.

What if he found out Ayla was about to harm him and decided to do something terrible? *No!* She squeezed her eyes shut at the terrifying thought. No matter how much she thought about it, it would take much less time for Rodrigo to break Estella's neck than it would for Ayla to jump onto the balcony or burst through the door.

I have to wait until he steps away from Estella.

Upstairs, Ada and Kalen were thinking about the same thing. They had thrown an ax and waited for an opportunity to get rid of Rodrigo, but no such opportunity came.

Ada, Kalen, and Ayla all gnashed their teeth as they imagined dismembering Rodrigo, who had lured away their naive little sister.

"So, are you saying there's something you can do for me?"

"No, it's something we have to do together." I could tell he had let his guard down a bit by the calm tone of his voice.

Keeping an ear out for Kalen and Ada on the rooftop, I pulled Rodrigo further away from the railing. Carefully, I pushed him against the balcony door and stood before him. Since I was shorter than he was, I wouldn't be able to cover him with my body, but at least my siblings wouldn't be able to attack him as easily.

"I don't like asking questions. I am usually the one who answers them." Rodrigo crossed his arms, frustrated, as he pushed me to continue.

"I'll make it quick." I cleared my throat, ready to reveal my plans to him. Nothing particularly clever or grandiose, but it was a plan. In order to save him, I needed to stay close to him. And I knew the best—maybe the only—way to do so. *Why am I nervous?*

I took a deep breath and said, "Let's get married."

His face froze. We both waited, uneasy for a long moment of silence, until he demanded, "Is this a new Kartina tactic?"

I let out a laugh at Rodrigo's response. *I was being serious and everything.* I scoffed, "*Pfft.* What?"

"Is it a distraction tactic to attack me while I'm too shocked to react? Or to make me keel over from shock? Or are you trying to give me a heart attack?"

It was quite a mean response to a marriage proposal. I frowned. "That's a lot of questions for someone who doesn't like asking questions."

"Something completely unpredictable happened, you see."

"That's life."

"I never thought I'd get a life lesson from a Kartina."

I put my hand on Rodrigo's cheek again. "Didn't you say you were curious as to why I was doing this? Will you believe me if I tell you the reason?"

Rodrigo took my hand off his cheek. But he didn't let go of it.

I let him hold my hand as I looked up at him. He had to know. "Because I want to survive."

Estella's sudden marriage proposal and declaration that she wanted to survive had Rodrigo at a loss for words. The Kartinas were the ones who had been tormenting him all along, but Estella's words made Rodrigo feel like he was the villain.

"I'm asking you to take good care of me and my family when you gain power someday. I don't want to die, you see."

There was no indication of dishonesty in her words. The same was true for her solemn blue-green eyes. Estella definitely seemed like someone who was telling the truth.

Can I trust her?

Rodrigo began making calculations in his head. The gains and losses he would incur if he were to accept Estella's offer. It was an offer that would benefit him in every scenario. He would be able to block most attacks from the Kartinas through Estella, and the news of their relationship would get all those annoying women to back off, not to mention that the emperor wouldn't be able to walk all over him. With a series of intelligent and thorough calculations, the decision came quickly.

Rodrigo released Estella's hand. He leaned against the wall, making himself more comfortable. Before he gave her his answer, he took a good look at her.

Estella was as beautiful as the rumors had suggested. And so vastly different from the other Kartinas. He was sure that a fake relationship and a fake marriage would not do her any good.

"Just take my hand." Estella held out her hand. There was something about it that was strangely alluring and reliable.

And truth be told, Rodrigo was exhausted. He was surrounded by enemies. And formidable ones at that. Wouldn't it be all right for him to take her small hand, which promised to protect him, and finally get some respite?

"All right. Let's do it." Rodrigo convinced himself once again that he had nothing to lose.

"All right, when should we have the wedding?" Estella prompted.

"No, not marriage."

Estella tilted her head to the side, curious. Rodrigo put his hand on her cheek. Had her hair come loose while they were dancing or when she clung to him? A loose lock tickled the back of his hand.

Rodrigo slowly lowered his head. His lips stopped precariously close to the corner of her mouth. They were tantalizingly close. Estella drew in a breath.

The tension Estella felt was the kind any woman would feel in this situation. His face was a work of art, but the smile on it was something art couldn't imitate.

He's using his looks? Estella realized that all those seduction tactics she had learned were useless against a naturally stunning person like him.

"Shouldn't we start with dating? There is still a year left until you are of age."

Oh, right. You have to be an adult to get married. I had forgotten since age wasn't important to the Kartinas. *Is it because he's the male lead? He's playing by the book.*

"All right, let's do that." Estella moved to stand next to him, linking her arm with his. Archenemies to lovers.

The stage was set. The game of deception had begun.

It saddens me that I have to deceive my family, but it's for their own good. So it's okay... Everything will be okay. Estella smiled brightly as she drew open the curtains.

But soon after, Estella was disheartened. Having cleared the big hurdle that was Rodrigo, she had thought everything would be okay, but that optimism went down the drain as soon as they returned to the banquet.

The banquet ended in chaos.

Kalen, Ada, and Ayla could not conceal their astonishment when they saw me and *Rodrigo* emerging arm in arm from the balcony.

Forgetting that they were surrounded by people, Kalen started throwing the shuriken he had hidden in his clothes, as Ayla offered some poison to Rodrigo that she had quickly concocted. Right in front of him, in front of everyone, out in the open.

Ada took a moment to react, but then she pulled out her sword. The sounds of clashing blades broke out, accompanying the beautiful music played in the banquet hall.

Clang! Clang! Clang! Swords flashed and struck together. Tables toppled over, and all kinds of colorful expletives escaped Ayla's mouth.

Screams erupted here and there, but even then, the musicians were so absorbed in their performance that the music continued, and the combination of women screaming alongside the instruments was practically comical.

"Once I get my hands on you, you're dead!"

"You think I'm going to let you catch me?"

Rodrigo's reply sent Ayla over the edge. She set off a smoke bomb. The green smoke was enough to scare people off. The entire crowd began to scream and scramble over each other to get away. Duke Gloria had gone pale.

CHAPTER EIGHT

Amidst the chaos, Ada and Ayla raced to try and rescue me.

Rodrigo snatched me up and kicked off the walls three times, bringing me to the second floor.

"What was that?" *What a great technique. I should learn that!* As I asked this with sparkling eyes, Rodrigo's eyes crinkled.

"It's magic," he said.

Oh, no wonder... I knew those movements were superhuman.

The Kartinas were very skilled, but unfortunately, they didn't have any magical powers. Rodrigo and I stood next to each other and watched my siblings run up the stairs toward us.

"I've always thought this, but you Kartinas are really something."

Unlike the downstairs hall that was filled with green smoke, the air on the second floor was clear.

"Are you making fun of us?" I asked Rodrigo.

"No, I'm just impressed."

Nah, that sounded like he was making fun of us.

"Estella! Where are you, Estella?!" My siblings shouted.

"What did that rat bastard do to you? Is he blackmailing you, Estella?" followed by "I'll tear you apart, Rodrigo! Give me back my sister right this second!" This was accompanied by a series of expletives and threats so nasty that I wanted to wash out my ears.

"I feel like I made the wrong decision." Rodrigo said, arms crossed as he listened to the cursing. "I have a feeling that I'm closer to death than ever."

There's no way... right? I let out an awkward laugh but had to admit he was right only a few days later.

[Recently, the Kartinas sent bombs to destroy the eastern manor on my property. Thanks to you, we no longer need to demolish that building. I would like to express my gratitude.]

"What are you doing, Your Grace?" The expression on Gunther's face was one of unease as he questioned Rodrigo.

Rodrigo took his pen off the paper, looking up for a moment. "Can't you see that I'm writing? If you're tired, go home and rest."

"I may not be in my right mind right now, but it is not because I am tired." Gunther unfolded a newspaper and placed it on Rodrigo's desk.

The letter Rodrigo had been writing was covered completely.

"A Modern Romeo & Juliet: Is There Any Hope for the Love that Blossomed Between Two Warring Families?"

After the commotion at Duke Gloria's banquet last week, Estella and Rodrigo had been quick to announce their relationship. The capital was in an uproar. Rodrigo was overwhelmed to say the least. He had to visit the emperor to confirm the rumor and had to deal with assassins sent by the Kartinas on a regular basis.

And Estella... *I wonder where she is and what she's doing.*

The woman who had told him all those strange things, like promising to protect him or saying she wanted to stay alive, seemed to have disappeared as if she had never existed. *Is she in confinement by the Kartinas?*

Pausing to consider the Kartinas were irredeemable villains without mercy, Rodrigo frowned.

"The eastern manor was blown up." Gunther tapped a corner of the newspaper. It was a picture of a familiar manor, as well as a black spherical object falling onto it.

"Newspapers these days have great illustrations, don't they?"

"That's not the issue, Your Grace. Are you really going to court that Kartina?"

Rodrigo disliked being questioned. He especially hated being questioned about matters that were already settled. The fact that Gunther, who knew this, was questioning him regardless, was a sign of how much he disliked the situation.

"I cannot shake my suspicions about that Lady Estella." Gunther was aware of the peculiar deal between Rodrigo and Estella.

"Is that so?" Rodrigo asked.

"Yes, she tried to seduce Your Grace out of nowhere."

At Gunther's words, Rodrigo recalled Estella's actions that night. *Her mannerisms were definitely not seductive. The way she suddenly pulled and pushed me was more combative than anything.*

"And all that talk of marriage definitely points toward her targeting your money."

Money, eh? Rodrigo said, "The Kartinas are wealthy too, though."

Unable to refute this, Gunther went silent. Then, "But it really is suspicious, isn't it?"

Rodrigo got up from his seat. He balled up the newspaper and tossed it, then crumpled the letter underneath and threw that in the wastebasket too.

"While we're on this matter, Gunther."

"Yes, Your Grace." Gunther straightened up and waited for Rodrigo to continue.

Rodrigo's lips spread into a wide smile at Gunther's readiness to do whatever was commanded of him. "I want to visit the Kartinas," Rodrigo said, as if it was a casual afternoon walk, but Gunther tensed up.

An Erhart... visiting the Kartinas.

It had been nearly a century since that happened.

"Estella, just tell me. Did that man... blackmail you?"

My family had been pestering me all week. After returning from the banquet, I announced my relationship with Rodrigo. "*It was love at first sight. We're destined to be together.*"

Naturally, nobody believed this cliched development straight out of some third-rate romance novel. The Kartinas, very in character, believed that Rodrigo had found leverage and used it to blackmail me.

"*There's no way Estella has any sort of weak point to exploit.*"

"*The only thing our darling Estella can't do is kill people! She's perfect in every other way!*"

I even saw them refuting their own hypothesis. It was very frustrating.

In addition to my siblings, my parents, Hela and Stefan, also pestered me. Thanks to their constant pleas to reconsider and following me everywhere, I hadn't been able to contact Rodrigo at all after parting ways with him a week ago without so much as a proper goodbye.

I don't even have time to write a single letter.

As soon as I woke in the morning, three pairs of teary eyes greeted me at the foot of my bed. Mealtimes were as quiet as a funeral, and all lessons and training had been put on hold. Everyone was trying to persuade me.

"You're wrong. Sir Rodrigo is a good man."

"Estella... that can't be true. Those dirty Erharts have always..." And so began Stefan's long-winded retelling of the history of the two families.

The enmity between the Kartinas and the Erharts could be traced back to ancient mythology. The Goddess Illia had loved a man full of greed. His name was Phalemon, and he wished to conquer and unite the continent under his rule. Illia, in love with him, wanted to help.

"What is it that you want?" she had asked.

"I want power," came his answer.

Illia gave him three dragons. One crimson, one black, and one blue. Phalemon also had loyal comrades behind him. The continent was too vast for one individual to conquer by himself. Phalemon gave two of the dragons Illia had gifted him to his friends. He kept the red dragon and gave the black dragon to Kartina. The blue dragon was given to his half-brother Erhart. According to mythology, these three conquered the continent together and established the empire. And Phalemon claimed the title of emperor.

Peace did not last long.

Having obtained power and authority, the three men could no longer trust each other. In the end, the three houses began to fight amongst themselves.

From here on out, the legend differed according to the Kartinas and the Erharts. The Kartinas claimed that Erhart had launched a surprise attack and killed their dragon. The Erharts, on the other hand, claimed that Phalemon allied with the Kartinas to kill *their* dragon and to drive his family to the brink of annihilation.

In any case, the feud between the two families began with this mythology.

And the Kartinas were taught this story from birth.

"The Erharts are our enemies." Even if there were other foes along the way, the main enemy was always them. The Erharts.

This belief that they had been indoctrinated with since birth was not easily swayed. And the emperor also made sure to toss them a few scraps to keep fighting over.

This is why indoctrination is scary. I started thinking about other things as I pretended to listen to Stefan's story about how terrible the Erharts were. *Rodrigo will probably be left alone for a while since the Kartinas are so focused on me, right?*

That was the bright side, but it was only that afternoon that I found out how wrong I was.

Kaboom!

The explosion was followed by the clatter of rock fragments spraying across the ground. The smoke billowed up, all the way to the fourth floor, where my bedroom was.

Dirt and rock were strewn everywhere, and the trees that had just begun to blossom had been snapped in half like twigs.

"What's all this commotion?" Stefan shot up from where he had been sitting, holding my hand, telling me about the Erharts' misdeeds.

"Master!" My bedroom doors were thrown open to reveal a knight, completely out of breath. "The Erharts have invaded us!" He collapsed with an arrow stuck to his side.

The small flag at the end of the arrow shaft seemed to wave at me in greeting. On it, Rodrigo's blue dragon crest was clearly visible.

"Everybody, get to your positions. Find out how many troops Erhart has."

Is Rodrigo insane? Is this his idea of dating? Everyone's already against it, and now he's challenging them to a fight. I let out a deep sigh.

"Estella, this is for the best. If he has somehow found out about some weak point of yours that you wanted to keep secret even from us, it would be better to dispose of him discreetly."

The news that an Erhart had entered the Kartina property must have already reached the capital. Many eyes watched both the Kartinas and the Erharts, after all.

Ayla and Ada, who had misunderstood why I was sighing, patted my shoulders reassuringly. The corners of their eyes trembled slightly.

You guys are enjoying this, aren't you?

"We'll be back, so don't leave your room." My family exchanged looks and steeled their resolve as I stood there, bewildered.

Defeat the Erharts.

Am I supposed to be happy that the Kartinas are united over a common goal? Kalen ran out of the room first, to secure the best position for throwing his shuriken.

"That's cheating, Kalen!" Ada was hot on his heels.

In the blink of an eye, my room was empty. I waited, assuring everyone had run off before I climbed out of bed.

Bending down, I stuck my arm under the bed and groped around. *I swear I left it here... Aha!*

A quiver of arrows. Rodrigo may be powerful, but it would be hard even for him to deal with all of the Kartinas at once. On top of that, this was the Kartina manor. I would support Rodrigo from the shadows. To protect my family too.

I swung open my bedroom window and peered out, spotting Rodrigo almost immediately. The wind dissipated the billowing smoke. Rodrigo, who marched across the destroyed garden, was unnecessarily good-looking.

He wasn't alone. Two knights strode beside him. That was all. I let out an exasperated laugh. *Did they seriously come here, just the three of them? Irritating. Does he need to get his ass kicked to realize how scary the Kartinas are?*

My hand, holding an arrow, dropped to my side. At that moment, I heard a strange laugh that sounded like a battle cry. It was Ada. *Ada with her sword!* The little hairs on my arms stood on end.

Ada was a sword master. If she wanted to, she could cut a small house in half, easily.

As I looked down from my bedroom, I knew she was ready to go all out. A light aura emanated from her hands. Near Ada, Kalen steadied himself on one of the trees that were still standing, brandishing his shuriken.

It's still two against three. And Rodrigo was extremely skilled as well. He'll be fine without my help.

A flash of color caught my eye. Seeping yellow gas spreading across the ground.

Poison! Hela and Ayla released poison!

CHAPTER NINE

How many people would be prepared for a poison cloud attack? I was worried about Rodrigo and his men. I knew what kind of poison they were facing.

I quickly examined Ada and Kalen from afar. They were busy swinging their swords and throwing shuriken, and neither of them was wearing a mask.

It's definitely the poison our mother made.

The Kartinas' specialty poison. We had been continuously exposed to Hela's uniquely crafted poison. It was a kind of training for us to develop a tolerance against it. The Kartinas were therefore immune to the otherwise lethal poison cloud heading toward Rodrigo.

I rummaged through my drawer. After being reborn as a Kartina, I had taken on the role of making sure that the Kartinas did not commit greater misdeeds. Because of this, I had been developing an antidote to counter Hela's poison.

Hastily, I searched for the antidote for the reeking yellow poison cloud. I skimmed through the leather pouch that held various bottles of medicine. "Here it is!"

I fished out a bottle filled with a clear liquid sloshing inside the glass. *Is it really this one?*

I opened the lid and sniffed. The notes of citrus confirmed that this was indeed the antidote for the poison cloud outside. I tied the small bottle securely to an arrow.

After writing "Drink this immediately, E" on the lid, I moved to the window to draw my bow. I aimed at the empty space just past Rodrigo's shoulder.

It had to miss him by a tiny margin. If the arrow went too far, he wouldn't notice it, and if it was too close, he could get hurt.

I took a deep breath.

Noting the direction of the wind, I reminded myself that in my past life, I had been a descendant of Jumong, famous for his archery skills, and released the bowstring.

Rodrigo readied himself to dodge the arrow heading toward him, but he froze. Something attached to the arrow had glinted in the sunlight. But that's not why he didn't dodge it. The reason Rodrigo changed his mind was the blonde hair fluttering in the breeze in the distance, where the arrow had come from. A woman with bright blonde hair, like strands of gold.

Estella.

"Watch out, Your Grace! An arrow!" Gunther shouted, but Rodrigo held up his hand to activate his magic.

The arrow came to a halt right by Rodrigo's shoulder, and he read the attached note. It was indeed from Estella. The corner of his lips rose into a smirk. *No wonder they're pulling their punches. They used poison. As expected of the Kartinas.*

Poison clouds weren't usually part of a sword fight. Poison was the last resort. *And they're starting the fight with it?* It was incredibly underhanded.

With no suspicion whatsoever, Rodrigo took a sip from Estella's medicine bottle and handed it over to Gunther and Devlon.

"Drink this."

"Who is it from?"

"My lover." Rodrigo grinned widely as he brandished his sword. "All this effort just to see my girl." *Look at all these obstacles in my way.* Rodrigo clicked his tongue as he raised his sword.

"Sir Rodrigo!" Once Rodrigo reached the front door, I shouted for him and entered the scene.

Five Kartinas surrounded Rodrigo and his two knights. As I witnessed the way Rodrigo's smile didn't falter, even at knifepoint, I felt like my worries had been wasted.

"Estella." His voice was soothing and kind. It was enough to shake all the Kartinas who were present.

"Everyone, stop!" I pretended to be agitated. And then I pushed aside Stefan, shocked at my tone, and ran toward Rodrigo. To create a dramatic scene.

As I pushed off the ground and jumped, he opened his arms wide and caught me in an embrace. A puff of dirt and dust came off his clothes. Holding back a cough, I hugged him as tightly as I could—as if reprimanding him for all the commotion.

"Estella, that man is..." Stefan trailed off, staring at me clinging to Rodrigo.

Hela and my siblings had a similar reaction. As if they were facing death, they were as pale as a sheet.

Rodrigo snickered as he hugged me back. He must have found the Kartinas' reaction amusing. He lifted his hand and stroked my hair for them to see, crooning, "I missed you, Estella." A cringeworthy line for good measure.

I could practically hear everyone's hearts sinking all the way down to their feet. When I lifted my head slightly, I caught sight of their devastated faces. Due to the sudden heavy atmosphere, the Kartina servants found themselves tiptoeing around, unable to approach.

A moment of silence hung heavy in the air. Rodrigo's two men eyed their surroundings during the deathly hush. Another battle had begun, a silent, invisible one.

I had witnessed the Kartinas commit countless evils, but I had never been afraid of them. But the frigid glares of the Kartinas, sharp and cold like ice, at this very moment were a little, no, a great bit frightening.

Amidst the razor-sharp edges of the Kartinas' glares, the eerie silence continued. *I guess I'm the only one who can break this silence.*

"Sir Rodrigo," I said, startling the others out of their quiet. "Thank you for coming."

"No, Estella. You agreed to call me Rodrigo."

I lifted my head, still in his embrace. *That's some first-rate acting. This is someone who will go from zero to a hundred in a heartbeat.*

Meeting my eyes, Rodrigo let out a chuckle. It was a sound that made my heart flutter just a bit. *Aha, I see. We're going all out, aren't we?*

I immediately understood what Rodrigo was trying to do. I pushed away from his chest with both hands. His jacket had been cut up during the battle, and the only thing separating me and Rodrigo was a thin shirt. His heartbeat was rapid, probably still fueled by adrenaline because of the fight.

"All right, Rodrigo. Since you're here, I want to properly introduce you to my parents." I stepped out of his embrace and slipped my hand into his.

Hela and the rest of my family were staring at me as if the world had ended. The question on all of their minds was clear: *Are you two really dating?!*

"I'm impressed by your hospitality." Rodrigo wasn't just sweet-talking. We were seated in the reception room, and he and I sat next to each other while Stefan and Hela sat facing us. Hela and Stefan seemed to have forgotten the commotion moments ago and were calling for the butler to prepare something for our guest with all the grace of a generous host.

Soon, a line of servants entered the room, bringing in refreshments, tea, and other drinks. A tower of macarons occupied one corner of the large coffee table, alongside a valley of chocolates, various floral teas, and fresh fruits. If it weren't for their tattered, battle-worn clothes, it would have looked like a perfect tea party.

"Since you have entered the premises, we might as well treat you well before we decide to kick you out. Isn't that right, Your Grace?" Stefan addressed Rodrigo politely, aiming to prevent any nitpicking of his words. It was Stefan's way of showing he wasn't letting his guard down.

"Go ahead. The tea is getting cold." Hela said as she pushed the teacup toward Rodrigo, her long sleeve briefly brushed over it.

I was certain. *She poisoned it.*

But Rodrigo seemed to suspect nothing as he reached out to take the offered tea. I realized why Rodrigo was always in danger. He was careless enough to drink the tea offered to him by his enemies. *If he's that trusting, it seems like it won't be easy to protect him.*

Under the table, I lightly kicked Rodrigo's foot.

Rodrigo turned his head toward me. Smiling brightly, I wiggled my eyebrows. *That tea you're about to drink is poisoned!* I glared at him. The Rodrigo who stroked my hair for everyone to see by the front door should be able to understand.

"What is it, Estella? You want me to hurry up and try the tea?"

Despite my signal, Rodrigo simply smiled and willingly lifted his teacup. For a moment, I was in despair. *He's so clueless.*

There was definitely poison in Rodrigo's tea. If I knew what kind of poison it was, I wouldn't be so anxious about him drinking it since I could just give him an antidote. But I had no idea what poison Hela had added to the tea. It would take too long to find the right antidote, which meant that there would be lingering effects even after the poison was neutralized.

The Kartinas were digging their own graves.

I sent Rodrigo another pleading look, trying to dissuade him from drinking it, but he simply gave me an odd smile.

"Thank you, Countess Hela." The teacup reached Rodrigo's mouth. His scarlet lips parted.

Without hesitation, I threw myself at his side. "Rodrigo, it's been so long! What have you been doing all this time without me?"

His hand swayed, and he quickly moved it away from me to prevent the spilling tea from reaching me. Rodrigo's eyes crinkled.

Rodrigo knew his tea was poisoned. How could he not, when Estella was clearly panicking? The reason he had tried to drink the tea anyway was because he wanted to see what Estella would do, and most of all...

"E-Estella, did you just hug that bastard?"

"Estella..."

He wanted to see how the Kartinas would react. It was amusing to watch the Kartinas rendered speechless as they looked at their daughter in despair.

"Oh my! I nearly forgot. I said I would introduce you formally to my parents."

Estella plucked the teacup out of Rodrigo's hand and placed it on the table. Acting as if she hadn't just thrown herself at him like a woman desperately in love, Estella straightened herself like a modest noblewoman and scooted a respectable distance away from him.

How amusing.

Rodrigo made great effort to suppress his smile and prepared himself to play along. "I've been busy, Estella. Things got hectic when the eastern wing of the manor was blown up."

Estella's gaze quivered at the mention of an explosion. She knew it wasn't simply an accident and that the Kartinas were behind it. Estella looked over at Hela and Stefan reproachfully. They avoided her gaze.

Of course. Estella let out a small sigh. "Mom, dad, everyone."

When Estella addressed them with a stony expression, the Kartinas tensed up. Estella was always smiling—except on very rare occasions when she was absolutely furious. That was why the Kartinas were nervous. *Our darling Estella is scary when she's angry.*

"This is the man I love."

At Estella's firm tone, Stefan and Hela's expressions were doused in despair. Her siblings reacted in much the same way. And soon, that despair morphed into fury directed at Rodrigo. *That goddamned Erhart seduced our innocent Estella!* Five pairs of blazing eyes glared daggers at Rodrigo.

Rodrigo remained silent, smiling.

Ada and Ayla fumed. *That's not the right attitude for someone who wants to court our precious Estella!*

CHAPTER
TEN

A man formally introducing himself to the family of the woman he loved, especially if the family was opposed to the relationship, should be on his hands and knees explaining himself and begging for their approval, but Rodrigo shamelessly sat there, doing nothing.

He's making Estella do all the talking!

Shameless bastard.

The fork in Ada's hand bent out of shape. Putting the now-useless fork down, Ada picked up a knife instead. It was a simple utensil, but in the hands of a Kartina, it was a lethal weapon.

"Don't torment this man ever again," Estella said quickly. Ada's grip on the knife loosened.

"We didn't blow up the manor," Kalen quickly added, fearing that Estella would hold a grudge.

"Of course *you* didn't." *You're not an explosives expert.*

They blew up a manor on the Erhart estate, basically a declaration of war. If the Erharts had arrived with their full military force, the Kartinas wouldn't be able to complain.

They were clearly in the wrong. Even if they hated the Erharts, it was wrong to start a war. It would be a different matter if it had been two average families fighting, but this was the Erharts and the Kartinas from the founding myth of the empire. In this case, the culprit would have to have been Stefan or Hela—someone who would be able to handle a full-on war.

"Oh, Estella. I found this at my house. It seems like it belongs to the Kartinas, so I took good care of it and brought it here." Rodrigo held his hand out to Gunther. The luxurious box shimmered, polished and covered in shiny jewels.

Rodrigo held the box out to Estella, and her face froze.

The box contained shuriken with many pointy edges, and there was no doubt that they belonged to Kalen. A regular shuriken has four tips. But Kalen's shuriken were made of sixteen sharp, pointed tips. Difficult to throw, but they were swift and lethal.

I was unable to hold back a sigh. It was obvious how much Rodrigo had suffered during the past week and why he came here today. He wanted me to hold up my end of the bargain. A deal's a deal.

I didn't want to resort to this, but I had no other choice. I didn't think my family would be so uncooperative. I lowered my head and bit my lip. My eyes filled with tears as I bit down hard enough to draw blood. When I looked up, I looked like a tragic heroine. "Please don't torment Rodrigo. If you do… it would break my heart."

Threatening to kill myself if they tormented Rodrigo would be most effective, but it might also backfire. There was a time for threats and a time for tears. I forced out a sob and buried my face in Rodrigo's chest. His body was trembling subtly. *He's definitely trying not to laugh.* I hoped that he knew I was doing my best to protect him.

Playing along, Rodrigo made a shushing noise and kissed the top of my head with a loud smack of his lips. I could practically hear the Kartinas scowl.

"What now? Estella was crying. Our darling Estella was shedding actual tears!"

The effect of Estella's single teardrop was impressive. The tea party had ended early, and Hela and Stefan had retreated to their bedroom without a word. Soon after, Odelle, the Kartina family doctor, dropped by.

Kalen, Ada, and Ayla had gathered separately.

"Pearly tears were flowing from my dear Estella's eyes!" Kalen clenched his fists tightly, unable to calm down.

In actuality, Estella hadn't shed any tears. She wasn't good enough at acting to cry on command. The most she could do was get her eyes to well up, but that wasn't what it had looked like to her siblings. In their memory, Estella sobbed and cried endless tears, her heart broken.

"It's all that bastard's fault! We have to get him away from her somehow! Our Estella is in distress because of that bastard Rodrigo."

Ayla tried to stand up with her sword in hand, but Ada stopped her. "Let's not do anything to make Estella sad again. She clearly told us not to torment that shameless bastard."

They had long since stopped referring to Rodrigo by name.

"What are we going to do, then?"

The three siblings fell silent, their expressions serious. The air tensed around them, their expressions and stances murderous.

"I've thought about this a lot. There's a reason that Estella fell head over heels for that useless asshole."

"What is it?"

Kalen said solemnly, "It's because Estella has no tolerance against men."

Kalen had expected to be told that he was spewing nonsense, but when Ada and Ayla continued to listen to him in all seriousness, he felt a bit awkward. Still, he was convinced his hypothesis made sense.

Estella was treasured by the Kartinas. Unlike her two older sisters, who had been sent out to flirt with all kinds of men to practice the art of seduction, Estella had been confined to the Kartina manor. No one besides her family and her personal servants was allowed to talk to Estella, and none of her servants were male—to ensure her beauty didn't put her in any danger.

As a result, before the ball Estella had never really met any men outside of her family members, their elderly butler, and the Kartina soldiers, who could not even look her in the eye.

"That's true. Estella is really innocent."

"You have to admit that vile beast has a nice face."

Ada and Ayla had to agree with Kalen. *That's right, our darling Estella is just too innocent. That's why.* "So what's your idea, Kalen?"

"Estella has to meet more people. Someone who has only met one trash person wouldn't be able to tell that they are trash."

"You want to introduce more men to Estella?" Ayla's voice cracked as she asked this. Would that really be the lesser evil? *I only want good things for Estella...*

"No, we should show her what a trash person is like. Then she'll be able to recognize trash when she sees it. All men except me and dad are trash when it comes to Estella, anyway," Kalen muttered.

"You have someone in mind, don't you? You have a plan?" Ayla asked.

Truth be told, he didn't. The Kartinas believed that the best laid plans were no plans at all. Even if something went wrong, they had the ability to take care of the consequences themselves, so they had no need to go through the bother of making plans.

As Kalen hesitated, Ada, who had been listening quietly, got up from her seat. "There can't be any negative consequences."

"Hm?"

"So it has to be someone higher up than an archduke."

Kalen stroked his chin as he considered this. Someone more powerful than an archduke... then... "You don't mean that son of a bitch crown prince, do you?"

Calling the crown prince a son of a bitch was something only a Kartina would do.

"That fool Detheus?" Ayla also shook her head.

Detheus, Imperial Phalemon. The Crown Prince of the Phalemon Empire was known to the people as the Crown

Prince of Light and was next in line to become emperor, but those like Kalen, who saw behind the facade, knew him as a fool and the worst delinquent of the century.

"You know how terrible he is!"

"I do. I also know how easily he falls in love. And how quickly he loses interest. He's exactly the kind of trash person you were talking about." Ada's plan was as follows: she would introduce Estella to Detheus, confident that he would undoubtedly fall in love with her. After all, Estella's incredible beauty and charm were hard to resist. *Actually, is there anyone in the empire who wouldn't fall in love with her at first sight?* Having fallen in love at first sight, Detheus would then do everything in his power to win her over. Estella would then realize that there were men who would revere her and fulfill her every wish, unlike that bastard Rodrigo.

But what if Estella fell for Detheus? All they had to do then was tell her about his many exploits with women. Detheus' history with women was enough to make any saint run away crying.

"Rodrigo... is pretty clean on that front."

"What a pity..." Ada mumbled to herself, then turned to the others to ask what they thought of her plan.

They weren't happy about it, but Kalen and Ayla agreed to it. It wasn't like they had any other options. By their standards, it was a carefully weighed decision. And, befitting the Kartinas, this plan was put into action lightning fast.

"Did you say Kartina?" Detheus had been stroking the naked side of a woman asleep on her stomach in the bed next to him when he paused and raised an eyebrow.

"Yes, Your Highness. Sir Kalen of the Kartinas has requested to see you."

"What does he want, so suddenly?"

Unable to answer the question, the servant averted his eyes.

"He avoided me whenever I asked him to visit. So why does he suddenly want to come to the palace?" Detheus' question wasn't directed at him, but the servant began to sweat nervously. "When does he want to see me?"

The servant was glad to finally be able to provide an answer. He said, "This afternoon, Your Highness."

As soon as he heard this, Detheus got up from the bed. His movement was enough to wake the sleeping woman, who tossed and turned. Detheus looked over at the small frame of the woman, who mumbled sleepily, and scowled. He raised his large hand and slapped the woman's naked back. *Slap!* The servant flinched at the sharp sound.

"Kyaaa!"

The woman let out a yelp at the sudden pain and sat up.

"Get out, now."

Confusion marred her face, but she didn't have time to hesitate. Detheus was about to raise his hand again. He said, "An important guest is coming. See to the preparations."

At Detheus' words, the servants began to make themselves busy.

Stark naked, Detheus leisurely crossed the room toward the windows. "A Kartina wants to see me, eh?" He stroked his chin, and his lips spread into a pleasant smile. At the same time, he clenched and unclenched his hands repeatedly. *I want the Kartinas in my grasp.*

The desire hidden deep within his heart reared its head. The Kartinas only took orders from the emperor. They never listened to anyone else. Even the crown prince. This was because there was no guarantee he would actually be able to ascend the throne. But on the other hand, whoever the Kartinas supported had a much higher chance of becoming emperor.

Detheus had two younger siblings. One sister and one brother. The crown princess had no right to the throne and was therefore no threat, but he needed to be wary of his brother. It was why he had made every effort to try and get the Kartinas on his side, but to no avail. Stefan was hard to meet in the first place, and Kalen, who was his age, kept his distance. But now Kalen wanted to see him, unprompted.

Detheus would give the Kartinas whatever they wanted.

CHAPTER
ELEVEN

Ayla and Ada had been pestering me since the morning and forced me to get on the carriage. The moment I got on, I knew I would soon regret it.

"It has been too long, Your Highness."

And, as expected, I did.

Kalen bowed with impeccable manners. Detheus smiled brightly as he approached him. "There's no need for such formality between us."

Between us?

Ayla and Ada exchanged glances. *Has Kalen been going around doing obscene things while we were not with him?*

"How gracious of you to treat me as a friend when we have only met briefly at a few banquets." Kalen made sure to clarify things for Ada and Ayla so there wouldn't be any misunderstanding.

"You're an exception. Who would want to miss a chance to get to know the Kartinas even if you've only greeted them in passing?" Detheus' reply was slick.

"These are my younger siblings."

Ayla and Ada took turns curtsying. Detheus' gaze moved steadily sideways before fixing on me. His eyes narrowed. His eyes said it all.

That he had fallen for me at first sight.

Damn it.

There's something I need to explain here. I wasn't being vain. He just falls in love really easily. Detheus' gaze focused on the beauty mark by my eye. If this had been my past life, I would have immediately gone to a dermatologist to have it removed.

"Who..."

"I am Estella of the Kartinas." I answered Detheus carefully, with an indifferent tone, just enough to avoid offending him. I would've rather not told him my name at all. I despised Detheus because I had read all about the horrible ways he treated women in the story. If Kalen had told me we were meeting Detheus, I would have pretended to faint just to avoid coming here.

"I did not know such a beauty was among the Kartinas. You are very beautiful, my lady."

Detheus took a step toward me, reaching for and grabbing my hand. My siblings' eyes widened as he leaned over and attempted to kiss the back of my hand. Nobody had expected the crown prince to be so bold.

The thought of Detheus' plump lips coming into contact with my body made me nauseated. *I hate this so much.* My body moved instinctively in response to this thought. I removed a tiny diamond shard from the brooch that held the ribbon around my waist in place and flicked my fingers.

"Gah!" Detheus let out a short yell and straightened up. He backed away, covering his eyes.

"Your Highness!"

Knights and servants alike quickly approached to check on him. His right cheek had a tiny wound that looked like he had been stabbed by a sharp needle. There was no blood, but it was enough of a spark of pain to shock him to his senses.

Who said you could touch me without permission?

If he weren't the crown prince, I would have shattered his wrist. *A shame, really.*

"It's fine, I'm all right. You can go."

"But Your Highness, your wound—"

"I said I'm fine! It's just a bug bite, stop overreacting," Detheus raised his voice.

"There must be a lot of bees in the palace gardens." I backed up Detheus' assumption, remembering to look concerned. The diamond shard had already fallen into the grass, making it impossible to find, and no one had seen a thing. No one would think I had attacked the crown prince. I wouldn't be suspected.

Changing my expression, I spoke softly to Detheus. "Your Highness, should you not rest inside if you are not feeling well?"

"No. It's just a bee sting, don't worry. There's no need," Detheus replied calmly.

"Your Highness, should we call the doctor?" The servants were particularly worried about Detheus today.

Detheus turned toward them and glared. "I told you all to back off."

You could practically hear him grinding his teeth. The servants and imperial guards distanced themselves.

"I've kept you ladies waiting," Detheus said, pretending to feel bad, and pulled out a chair for me, and only me. He slowly eyed me up and down, as if appreciating a magnificent work of art.

Is he insane? Does he need to lose his eyesight to come to his senses? I touched the bottle of poison in my pocket. *No, not this one. He'll die as soon as he ingests it.* I couldn't just kill the crown prince at the imperial palace, after all.

Detheus kept trying to talk to me. Judging by the lustful, yearning way he looked at me, he had definitely already fallen for me. Kalen and Ayla sighed.

Did you guys not expect this?

"I'm so glad to have tea with you," Detheus interrupted his staring at me long enough to tell Kalen.

"I see." Kalen's tone seemed bitter. I glanced over at my brother. I couldn't figure out why my siblings had brought me here. Were Kalen and Detheus close? At this point, anyone could see that Detheus was ogling me. I would have loved to gouge out his eyes, but that would have to wait. The sharp hook in my pocket was practically crying out.

"Lady Estella, you aren't eating anything. Is nothing to your liking?" Detheus, who had been talking with Kalen to save face, turned his body toward me. How could I possibly have an appetite when he was staring as if he was ready to devour me? He was not in his right mind.

It was broad daylight, and all my siblings were present, so it wasn't like he would try anything. Not that I'd let him, but the thought of the things he might do to me completely ruined my appetite. "No, no, Your Highness."

I didn't care to talk to him further, so I quickly picked up my teacup. The floral scent was quite excellent. They used the finest tea leaves, as expected of the palace.

Detheus' gaze fell on my pink mouth. He licked his lips, as if imagining something. Goosebumps traced up my arms and down my neck. I consciously avoided even looking in his direction. I simply hoped this visit would be over soon. Then—

"Estella, you should have told me you were coming to the palace. I would have sent a carriage for you." A chilly voice rang out. *Who is calling my name so tenderly yet with such a cold tone in broad daylight?*

I turned my head toward the voice. It was a familiar face. "Rodrigo?"

Why is he here? And with...

"Detheus! You have guests?"

...the princess?

Detheus' imagination ran wild as he watched Estella sip her tea. It had only taken one look at her crimson lips to stoke his desires. *I like what I see.*

Detheus tried to think of a way to send Kalen, Ada, and Ayla away so he could spend time alone with Estella. And just as he was starting to get frustrated by his lack of options—

"Estella, you should have told me you were coming to the palace. I would have sent a carriage for you."

An unwelcome voice, and...

"Detheus! You have guests?"

...a bright and familiar voice rang out.

Delia, Detheus' sister and the empire's princess, waved as she approached, smiling brilliantly. And next to her was Rodrigo, his brows creased in irritation.

"Delia, what brings you all the way here? It's been a while, Sir Rodrigo." Detheus made no attempt to hide his own disdain.

"The roses in your palace are much prettier. I wanted to show them to Sir Rodrigo." Delia tugged at Rodrigo's arm, pulling him along. He let her drag him around as she pleased.

Crack! A teacup shattered. It wasn't Estella's cup, but Ayla's.

"Oh my! You're soaked! Did the tea burn you? Oh dear." Delia fussed over it, and Estella quickly took out her handkerchief. Ayla shook her head before brushing the shards onto the ground as if nothing had happened.

"I apologize for breaking your expensive china. I got a little irritated." Ayla didn't hide the fact that breaking the teacup was no accident.

"Estella, I'd like to return home. I don't want to keep watching these horny sons of bitches drooling everywhere," Ayla whispered to Estella, obviously loud enough for everyone to hear.

Detheus scowled. It wasn't because of the "horny sons of bitches" comment. Detheus knew himself better than anyone, and could admit that the description was apt. What bothered him was the plural form she used when she said it. *So... there's someone other than me who is after Estella?*

"It's been a while, Your Highness. May the Goddess always be with you." Rodrigo slipped in a greeting in the middle of the commotion.

"Right, may the Goddess also—"

"Estella, what brings you to the palace? You didn't mention this in your letter yesterday. If I knew you were coming, I would have joined you or sent you a carriage." Before Detheus could finish his reply, Rodrigo lightly shook off the princess and stood in front of Estella.

The other horny son of a bitch was Rodrigo? Detheus forced a smile.

Also smiling, Rodrigo placed his hand on Estella's chin. His hand slowly slid from her chin up to her cheek. His eyes were cold, but his touch was gentle and warm. The contrast piqued Estella's curiosity.

What were you doing with the princess? More importantly, are you two close? I don't want to do all the work and let someone else take the credit. I was protecting Rodrigo and was to hand him over to the female lead safe and sound, not to the trashy princess. I said, "You never mentioned you're coming to the palace either, Rodrigo. If I had known, I would have joined you."

"Sorry, I got home late after visiting you yesterday."

"My parents did keep you there for a while. But you were quick to say goodbye to me."

I could see the corner of Detheus' lips twitching. Our conversation made it clear that we were more than just acquaintances. It was intentional, and our attitudes as well as the atmosphere between us practically spelled it out. Rodrigo and I were putting on our best performances to show that there was clearly something going on between us.

"Why don't you sit down?" Detheus' voice became dangerously low.

"We should be on our way." Ayla was already on her feet. She seemed infuriated by the fact that Rodrigo, who was courting her sister, had been gallivanting around the palace with the princess.

Ada was much the same. "We forgot we had to go take care of some monsters today, Your Highness."

The Kartinas were instrumental in the safety of the empire. They alone were responsible for taking care of the monsters that frequently spawned in the western borderlands. Just as in the founding myth, the Kartinas were still subservient to the Phalemons, and the two families supported one another. The Kartinas protected the empire from monsters, and the Phalemons turned a blind eye to the Kartinas' misdeeds. Detheus couldn't stop the Kartinas from leaving.

"Then I shall take my leave as well. Estella, should we at least leave the palace together?" Rodrigo held out his hand.

I was about to take it when Delia stepped between us.

She said, "Sir Rodrigo, won't you accompany me to the rose garden?"

CHAPTER TWELVE

Delia lifted her head to look up at Rodrigo with sparkling eyes.

What am I going to do with her?

Delia clung to Rodrigo's arm when he didn't react. She didn't see the way he frowned, and she continued pestering him, pulling his arm to swing it back and forth. "Sir Rodrigo, Sir Rodrigooo," she sang.

She was acting like an impolite little girl, but nobody tried to stop her. After all, Detheus was the only one who could reprimand the princess, and he enjoyed watching Rodrigo being put on the spot. At times like this, those who could intervene were not always those who had to.

"Your Highness."

Everyone's gazes turned toward me.

"Yes?" Delia responded with a tone that was decidedly different from before. Her coy and arrogant expression was similar to that of a mistress looking down at a concubine. It was irritating.

I'm the one he's dating. I thought Rodrigo and I had made our relationship clear with our earlier conversation, but it must not have been obvious enough for Delia. *Or maybe she's pretending not to notice?*

I said, "Sir Rodrigo and I have plans already." *We do?*

Rodrigo briefly raised his eyebrows before smiling graciously. *I like that he's clever.*

"That's right, Your Highness," Rodrigo said. "We agreed to introduce Estella to the servants at my mansion. Thank you for remembering, Estella."

Introducing me to the servants?

Introducing me to the servants, not to mention visiting each other's homes, implied that we were seriously discussing our future together. Delia's expression darkened. Delia was someone who, like a child, showed her emotions openly, but she did not demand that Rodrigo ignore a previous engagement in favor of entertaining her. *She was foolish, but not an idiot.*

"How about postponing it for a day?" Detheus was the rude one.

That tactless moron.

"The roses have bloomed beautifully, you see. Beautiful things tend to wither quickly. How about having another cup of tea in the back garden?"

Ayla and Ada wouldn't be able to stay with me. They had already made their annoyance apparent and talked about having to take care of monsters, so they had no choice but to leave. I looked over at Kalen.

"I shall stay. I can't leave Estella all alone."

"I'm all right, Kalen." I wanted Kalen to leave with the twins, but things didn't go my way. It would be hard to hold Delia in check while keeping an eye on Kalen, and I was ready to knock the princess out if she crossed a line. But if Kalen stayed behind, it would prove difficult to attack her.

"No, Estella. I won't go anywhere without you."

Please leave. I acted like I was touched and nodded.

"I guess that's that. What about you, Rodrigo?"

"If Estella is staying behind, I have no choice. I shall join you," he replied meekly, but the displeasure behind his response stung me.

Did you want to be alone with the princess? I can't allow that. Never. I would never approve of the princess, even if that meant keeping Rodrigo for myself.

When Detheus said the tea party was being moved to a different location, the servants got busy. We walked slowly to give them enough time to set up everything.

The field of roses at the back of the crown prince's palace was known as one of the most beautiful locations in the capital. Unlike other places, where roses bloomed and withered in May, Detheus' roses would bloom in May and last until the end of the harvest festival in October, thanks to magic.

"We could have seen them another day." Kalen's tone made it clear how annoyed he was. "Flowers that are artificially kept alive cannot be as beautiful as flowers that have bloomed on time naturally."

I could feel Detheus' gaze on me... and Rodrigo's too. There was something strange in the way Detheus eyed me. It was as if, somehow, he knew my relationship with Rodrigo was fake.

What in the world? I tilted my head slightly. The strong scent of roses greeted us before we even reached the flower field.

"Isn't the scent amazing, Sir Rodrigo?" Delia, attached to Rodrigo's side, chattered incessantly. Rodrigo responded to her every prompt, but his replies were short. Anyone, except Delia, could see that he was keeping her at arm's length.

Or she's pretending not to notice.

"He's not being a gentleman, Estella," Kalen whispered to me.

"What do you mean?"

"Rodrigo," Kalen said. "He's being so curt with the princess. He'll definitely treat you like that too."

Kalen seemed ready to criticize everything about Rodrigo, down to the way he breathed. His attempt to find fault with Rodrigo's mannerisms was admirable as a concerned brother. It was then that a little seed of suspicion began to sprout in my heart.

Was it a coincidence that Rodrigo appeared with the princess while I was with the crown prince? Me with Detheus, and Rodrigo with Delia. From the outside, both Detheus and Delia were good marriage candidates, after all. *Did Kalen have a hand in this? What a cute idea.* I had to laugh. Out of exasperation.

I told him, "Rodrigo isn't rude to me. He's actually extremely sweet." I tried to think of something incredibly lewd. *Come on, blush!* My efforts must have paid off because Kalen's gaze was shaking. *A round of applause for me and my impeccable impression of a blushing maiden in love.*

Thinking about the trouble I would go through trying to get Detheus off my back, it occurred to me that Kalen needed to suffer a bit as well.

"Wow! Look! Aren't they pretty? They're beautiful!" A wave of scarlet came into sight, causing Delia to beam and clap her hands like a child.

I halted too at the sight of the roses, glorious in full bloom. The beautiful scene tugged at my heart.

"Does it please you, Lady Estella?" Detheus noticed even the tiniest of reactions on my part.

"Yes, it's as beautiful as they say."

"If you'd like, I can send them to you."

And cut those beautiful roses? That was no good. I declined, "Everything has its appropriate place. Including people."

Taking a step away from Detheus, I moved to stand next to Rodrigo. *This is where I belong, so stop flirting.* In that moment, for their individual reasons, everyone fell silent—except, of course, for Delia.

After I had declined the gift of roses from Detheus, Delia tried yet again to converse with Rodrigo, but for some reason, he didn't even offer his short replies this time. It was out of character for him, usually such a gentleman.

The tea party continued in silence—other than Delia's background-noise chatter. Detheus still stared at me, eyes burning. Kalen let out a fake cough to signal his discomfort, but Detheus ignored him and said, "I prepared some rose tea for us to have in the rose garden."

As the silence began to weigh us down, Delia clapped her hands again, clearing the air. I felt bad for Delia, who was clearly trying to ingratiate herself to Rodrigo. *Come to think of it, wasn't Rodrigo Delia's first love?*

I remembered reading the sentence, *"The moment Rodrigo appeared in a black suit during Delia's birthday celebrations, he was carved into Delia's memory."* She said something like, *"I want Rodrigo to be mine, whatever it takes. As soon as I first saw him, everything else lost all meaning,"* and started to obsess over him.

For someone who had acted like a child her whole life and had never really had any strong wants, Delia's first desire bloomed at an alarming rate. And her desire was fervent.

Delia was the princess, and she was beautiful. She must have thought no man could reject her. They were technically related, but that was so far back in their family histories that the trace of relation in their blood was barely there at this point. Besides, the emperor approved.

All that was left was Rodrigo's answer, but then I suddenly popped up. She must be furious. I completely understood. But despite my existence, Delia seemed unwilling to give up on Rodrigo.

"I hear that young people date before getting married these days." Delia sounded like an old woman. I stared at her. "That's what I heard. Kalen, do you have someone?"

Kalen shook his head. I knew exactly where this was going. Delia and Detheus seemed to be trying to downplay the seriousness of my relationship with Rodrigo, making it sound like a mere passing fancy before marriage.

"Our mother's generation may have frowned upon dating before marriage, but it's just so common these days, you can't fault it. I find it quite sophisticated and admirable, actually. I hear men who take lovers before marrying treat their wives better." Delia continued cheerfully.

And you'd love to be that wife, huh? No way, not in a million years. I'm going to protect dear Rodrigo and hand him over to the heroine!

"Oh my, Sir Rodrigo, your teacup is empty. I'll pour you some more." Delia elegantly lifted the teapot.

"No thank you." Rodrigo immediately declined.

Embarrassed, Delia let out a little laugh and put the teapot down. She asked, "Rodrigo, are you not feeling well?"

"I think so, yes."

"Then you should go and get some rest." Detheus' response was lightning fast. Ever since Rodrigo had joined us, Detheus had been keeping an eye on him.

"No, Your Highness. It's just that the scent of roses is so strong, so I should be all right if I get some fresh air." Without waiting for Detheus' permission, Rodrigo stood up.

"Do you not like the rose scent? You should have told me..." Delia was close to tears. Rodrigo smiled faintly, but the tenseness of his jaw revealed annoyance. To anyone else, it might have looked like he was smiling good-naturedly, but I knew that was not it.

"That's not the case, Your Highness, so do not worry." Rodrigo gave a quick bow and walked away. Before leaving, he lightly brushed my shoulder.

Follow me. That's what his eyes said. I didn't get up right away. It would look strange if I followed him immediately.

"Lady Estella, I heard the Kartinas have to learn how to torture people?" Once Rodrigo was gone, I became Delia's target. The intent behind that innocent face was so obvious that I nearly laughed.

"Yes, of course," I said. "But I was never any good at it. I always cause trouble for my teachers." I gave a reasonable response to block Delia's attack, silencing her. *I can hear the gears moving in your head.* Before Delia could stop me, I got to my feet.

"Excuse me, may I use the lady's room?" I gave a strictly private excuse. After all, no one would stop me or accompany me to the bathroom.

"Where in the world is he?" I left the back garden and walked around the crown prince's palace. I had gotten quite far from the field of roses, but Rodrigo was nowhere to be seen. *If I*

had known this would happen, I would have asked where he was going.

"Did we miss each other? Should I go back?" Just as I was trying to decide what to do, a large hand emerged from the shadows and grabbed me.

"*Huff!*" I gasped and my hands, lifted instinctively in defense, made contact with a certain someone's solid chest. "Rodrigo!"

"You're late."

"It took me a while to find you." I added a bit of reproach to my reply. Rodrigo had been waiting in one of the corridors that connected the palace with the gardens and was used by the servants to move ingredients to the kitchens at dawn. Who could have known he'd be in a dark corridor that was rarely used during the day?

"We can't talk where people can see us," he whispered.

"Got something important to say to me?"

"Just some excuses and questions."

"What?" *What is he saying?*

CHAPTER
THIRTEEN

I had no idea how to respond, so I stood there, smiling with my mouth open.

"I shall start with my excuse. Today was the first time I met alone with the princess." Rodrigo spoke to me informally in front of others, but formally when we were alone. It was probably because two people in a relationship usually spoke informally with each other. On the one hand, I liked how polite he was to me when he was otherwise so brazen, but I also felt a little disappointed that it meant that he still might not trust me. More importantly, his excuse wasn't welcome.

I wasn't suspicious of him, anyway. I said, "I don't really mind."

"Is that so? I do. I would like to know why Crown Prince Detheus was staring at you like he was ready to pounce."

"I didn't think he was." I gave him a dismissive answer, not wanting to talk about Detheus, but that seemed to set him off. Rodrigo pulled at my hand that he was holding.

Thanks to him holding it up, I was forced to stagger a step closer to him.

He smiled. It was definitely a smile, but he didn't seem very happy. "Keep it in mind from now on. Those were the eyes of a fox eyeing prey."

The crown prince had been downgraded to a fox. I didn't point out the rudeness of his remark. When it came to insulting the crown prince, I had Rodrigo beat. *I had never insulted him out loud... but still.*

The wrist Rodrigo was gripping tightly began to ache, so I twisted it to try and break free. He was too close. His breath tickled my skin, and I could feel his warmth.

The narrow corridor was even more constricted in the shaded area. Still, there was no reason for him to stand this close to me. Rodrigo's grip on my wrist was as solid as a vice and wouldn't budge.

"Let go of my wrist," I demanded.

"I've given you my excuse, but I'm not done questioning you, you see."

"You could let go of me first."

"Then I wouldn't be able to see your eyes. It's already so dark."

"My wrist hurts," I snapped. I may be powerful and skilled, but it wasn't like my bones were particularly strong.

I was, of course, a bit sturdier than most people—since I was a Kartina.

"I apologize." He let go immediately and, instead, put his arm around my waist. He pulled me closer so gently that I didn't even think to react. I grabbed the hand touching my waist with mine.

His arms were strong from years of training. *I wouldn't be able to push him away even if I wanted to.* I gave up trying to break free from his embrace.

With his body glued to mine, he asked, "Who asked you to come to the palace?"

"My brother, Kalen," I said truthfully. His arm around my waist was sturdy and oddly comforting.

"Did you know you would meet Detheus?"

"No."

"Promise me not to come here ever again." Rodrigo said quite seriously.

"Are you worried I might cheat on you with Detheus?"

He let out a huff of laughter as if the idea was ridiculous. I leaned back to put a little distance between us. He asked, "Who do you think you are dating?"

"Rodrigo Duveli Erhart."

"Exactly."

As if to reward me for my reply, he tucked a stray strand of my hair behind my ear. I wanted to know the intention of his touch. As I was about to ask, I heard people talking. It wasn't like it would be terrible if we were seen, but I didn't particularly want strangers to see me in Rodrigo's embrace.

I took about half a step closer to him. He readily wrapped his arms around me until his large, black cloak covered both of us. Anyone passing by would think we were just part of the shadows.

The sound of footsteps did not come any closer and gradually grew faint.

A warm, pleasant scent emanated from him. Every time I took a breath and inhaled this warmth, my heart quickened its pace. For some reason, his breathing seemed to pick up as well.

"You may know my name but do not seem to know much about me, so let me tell you, Estella." He spoke with a long exhale that tickled the top of my head. "I do not allow my lover to cheat on me. At least not with a bastard like Detheus."

Is he trying to play the part? Could it be that he's jealous? More importantly, he was far too close, and it was getting hot.

"We've been gone too long," he said suddenly. "I'll go back first."

It really felt like being scolded by a lover. As soon as you fall too deeply into the role, the roleplay is over. I pushed him away. Rodrigo backed off, offering no resistance. As his large hand left my back, the breeze chilled me.

I missed his embrace, just a little.

"You took so long, Estella." Kalen was halfway out of his seat, about to get up. He added that he was just about to go look for me.

Great timing on my part.

"The palace is so spacious. It took me a long time just to find the bathroom." I fanned myself with my hand, playing the part of someone who struggled to find their way around. But I was flushed because of Rodrigo. *I'll have to tell him to change his perfume.* Kalen lifted my teacup and emptied it onto the ground before pouring me the cold drink that was provided.

"Drink this, Estella."

The iced drink finally helped calm my rapidly beating heart, and I took a few deep breaths. Still, thoughts of Rodrigo kept popping up. I was shaking my head to get him out of my mind when I felt a hot gaze on me. Detheus.

A fox eyeing its prey, huh? An apt description. Impressed by Rodrigo's way with words, I let out a fake little cough.

"Sir Rodrigo is taking so long. Something must have happened. I should go check." Just like how Kalen had been about to look for me, Delia stood up. Hearing the concern in her voice and her eyes, I could tell her affection was genuine.

Wait, I should have questioned him as well. Even though he had offered an excuse, in hindsight, I regretted not questioning him further. And the thought of the one-sided questioning irritated me a little. It stung thinking I was the one failing to hold up my end of the bargain while he was playing his role perfectly.

I wasn't professional enough. If the princess starts flirting with him again, I'm going to be more professional and put her in her place! I steeled myself.

And such an opportunity arose very quickly. Rodrigo returned, and Delia's expression cleared like the sky after heavy rainfall. She approached Rodrigo and tried to take his hand.

This is my chance. To act like his lover. I quickly skimmed my surroundings. *Something to throw, something to throw...* I could have used another jewel, but the two of them were in bright daylight. Kalen might notice if I threw something that glinted in the sun.

So instead, I dropped my fork onto the ground. A servant standing by quickly approached to pick it up for me, but I held out a hand to stop him and bent down to pick it up myself, along with a small rock.

Quick decisions, quick actions—like a true Kartina.

"Sir Rodrigo, where have you been? Are you feeling better now?" Delia raised her hand and placed it on Rodrigo's left cheek.

Without hesitation, I surreptitiously flicked the rock toward her. It hit a branch of the hepao tree that shaded Delia. A couple of birds flew up, causing several ripe hepao fruit to fall onto Delia's head.

"Eek!" Startled, Delia backed off, but it was too late. She was already a mess. The hepao fruit had exploded upon impact and covered Delia in black juice.

"Your Highness!" Delia's maids quickly approached her and started wiping her face as she stood there, dazed. Rodrigo, who had stepped away as soon as the branch shook, was spotless. He looked over at me.

What? Why?

I held his gaze and got up from my seat. "Are you all right, Your Highness? It looks like we should postpone our tea party. Ah—"

When I tried to step closer to Delia, Rodrigo grabbed my wrist and yanked me back. *Is he just strong or good at surprise attacks?* I mumbled as he pulled me into his arms.

Please, stop grabbing my wrist.

"What are you—"

"The ground is covered in hepao fruit, Estella. We can't have your shoes getting dirty."

Look at this man, worrying about his lover's shoes when the princess in front of him is covered in fruit...

"S-sir Rodrigo..." Delia was close to tears and obviously desperate for Rodrigo to console her. But Rodrigo's gaze was fixed on me.

How embarrassing.

"Ahem, I think we should get going, Your Highness." Kalen spoke up just in time. He glared at Rodrigo's hand holding my wrist as if ready to cut it off, before putting down his teacup and getting to his feet.

"It's so difficult to have tea with the Kartinas." At Detheus' pointed words, Kalen simply smiled.

"The Kartinas are always difficult. I'm a Kartina myself, but I don't always understand them." Kalen seemed irritated.

Is it because of Rodrigo? But why is he taking it out on Detheus?

"Thank you for the tea. We'll make sure to return the favor." Kalen easily jumped over the patch of fallen hepao fruit and held his hand out to me. "Let's go home, Estella."

"I'll escort you." As soon as Kalen finished his sentence, Rodrigo chimed in.

"No, that's unnecessary. I shall provide you with my carriage. Since I feel bad for today not going well." Detheus approached, and I was suddenly surrounded by three men. Delia had been long forgotten by all of them.

I was facing a dilemma. Rodrigo and I were currently acting like we were madly in love. It made the most sense to go with Rodrigo, but I felt bad for Kalen. He was my brother, and a doting one at that... *He'll be hurt if I refuse him, right?* Detheus was, of course, not even in the running. I took a moment to think, frowning. *Oh!*

I had a brilliant idea.

I smiled brightly and said, "What if you join us in our carriage, Rodrigo? You can introduce me to your servants at a later time."

That way, Rodrigo could escort me while I also took up Kalen's offer to go with him.

I was pleased with my ingenious solution, but then the crown prince spoke up.

"I would like you to take my carriage," he said.

Both Kalen and Rodrigo furrowed their brows, but Detheus paid them no mind. It was as if he only had eyes for me. Three pairs of eyes studied me.

One gaze was desperate, another slimy, and the third unfeeling but slightly threatening, complicating my dilemma even further. Coming to the palace had been easy, but leaving it was definitely not.

FOURTEEN

Inside the crown prince's carriage, I sat next to Kalen as Rodrigo sat across from us. This situation didn't make any sense. The silence inside the carriage was deafening. Kalen had been scowling at Rodrigo during the entire ride, and Rodrigo was staring out the window, seated comfortably and completely ignoring Kalen.

The two of them were statuesque, handsome, and unmoving. I was almost worried they had stopped breathing.

"Disgusting." It was the first word Kalen had spoken inside the carriage, and he spit it like fire. He might have overlooked Detheus' adamant insistence on forcing them into his carriage, but he didn't understand why he had to share a carriage with Rodrigo. Or maybe he just didn't want to understand.

"That idiot is tactlessly interrupting our time together," Kalen whispered into my ear.

"Kalen." I called his name in a quiet, reprimanding tone. I couldn't ask him to try and get into Rodrigo's good graces, but I couldn't just let him keep digging his own grave either.

"All right, Estella. I'll stop." Kalen's expression melted into a smile as if he hadn't just been furious. Silence fell again. A headache creeped up on me as I watched him sit there like a statue again. I let out a sigh and put a hand to my forehead.

The carriage rattled and shook. I was dislodged from my seat and, before I could even balance myself, Rodrigo and Kalen moved simultaneously. They reached out and grabbed me for support at the same time.

"Ha!"

"Hm."

And as their eyes met, they glared at each other with obvious animosity. They were each holding onto one of my arms rather tightly, as if in a game of tug of war, and they were both unnaturally strong.

Are they about to tear me in half? "Kalen, Rodrigo. That hurts."

It was only after I expressed my discomfort that they flinched and started to let go, but even then, it took a while. Neither of them wanted to let go first.

"Let go first," Kalen growled.

"It would be better if you let go of her." Rodrigo didn't back down either.

This is so childish. I said, "Let go at the same time."

The solution was like Solomon's. The two men eyed each other as if waiting for the other to act first.

"One, two, three!" In the end, I had to start counting down to escape their grasps. Rodrigo and Kalen let go of me and sat back down. This happened several times, thanks to the uneven road. *If I were emperor, I'd prioritize paving the roads. Ouch.*

Before we knew it, we arrived at the Kartina manor.

"Stop the carriage," Kalen ordered as he knocked on the side of the carriage closest to the driver. We had arrived at the entrance.

"Why don't you leave now?" Kalen suggested to Rodrigo.

"I would like to accompany you inside and at least greet Count Kartina since I'm here already."

Unaffected by Kalen's rudeness, Rodrigo made sure to observe proper etiquette. Kalen's face burned redder and redder. It seemed like he would start throwing shuriken inside the carriage if I let this continue. I had no choice but to put a stop to it.

"You should go home for today, Rodrigo."

"Shall I, Estella? Are you tired?" Rodrigo immediately backed down. Kalen clicked his tongue in an exasperated manner. "Then I'd like for us to talk for a moment."

"Just the two of you?" Kalen glared at him.

"Yes, just the two of us."

"No, never!"

Rodrigo ignored Kalen and looked at me. He was asking me what I was going to do. There was no way he was asking me to stay behind for no reason. I agreed to Rodrigo's proposition, saying, "Kalen, it won't take long. I'll be inside soon."

In exchange, I made the cutest face I could muster. I clasped my hands together, raised my eyebrows, and puffed up my cheeks a little. Ever since we were kids, Kalen had been unable to say no to this face. Today was no different. Kalen's lips twitched before he let out a sigh.

"Estella, if anything happens, just scream."

Rodrigo raised his eyebrows.

"Don't worry, Kalen. Thank you for being on my side." I lightly leaned my forehead against Kalen's shoulder. His face reddened in a different way from before. He seemed moved. *Have I neglected Kalen too much because of Rodrigo? I should pay more attention to him.* Kalen delayed his departure, seemingly still unwilling to leave the carriage.

"Kalen, are you really that eager to spend more time with Sir Rodrigo?" As soon as I said this, Kalen left the carriage. Silence again. I was finally able to breathe comfortably. Not only did I have to act all lovey-dovey with Rodrigo, but I was nervous that Kalen would attack Rodrigo at any second. *At this rate, I might die of a nervous breakdown before Rodrigo has a chance to kill me.*

"You look tired."

I gave a vague nod and prompted him, "Say what you have to say."

I glanced out the window. *Could Kalen be eavesdropping?*

But my worries were unfounded. Kalen was standing some distance away from the carriage. Glaring in our direction all the while.

"I don't have anything to say," he responded.

"What?"

"I was just a little irritated."

I didn't ask any follow-up questions. Not just because I was exasperated and baffled, but because I thought I knew what irritated him.

"It felt like my patience was being tested today."

"Did something happen?" I wondered.

"I had to do some things I don't like."

"What things?" I probed further, rather curious.

"Would you like to know?"

If you're going to say something, don't stop midway. Of course, I wanted to know. When I nodded, he began explaining. His calm and quiet tone was nice to listen to. And listening to him tell me about himself instead of reading about him on a page wasn't bad either.

"First thing in the morning, I received an order to go to the imperial palace. I thought there was an emergency, but the emperor simply told me to go and see Princess Delia."

So, the emperor has his eye on Rodrigo.

"Does that bother you?"

I must have frowned without realizing it for him to ask this. I said, "No, go on. It sounds like something I should be aware of."

"The emperor has asked me in the past what I thought of Princess Delia. Of course, I told him I had no interest in her."

"What exactly did you tell him? His Majesty is not one to give up so easily."

He's overly sensitive when it comes to his children, after all.

"I said I had no interest in women. He didn't bring it up again after that. But it seems to have started again."

"Why?"

"Do you really not know?"

I wouldn't ask if I didn't, you know. I shook my head.

"Because of the scandal between you and me. He must have thought the princess had a chance as well, now that my claim about having no interest in women has been disproven.”

It must have felt bad to spend time with a person who can't give you what you want. I told him, “I understand. Today must have been hard for you.”

“There was something else that irritated me.”

“There’s more?” *So temperamental.*

“The way Detheus looked at you. I hate it.”

“That’s not my fault.” I leaned back a little, feeling like I was being interrogated again, like I had been at the palace.

“Do not smile like that.”

I looked at Rodrigo, my eyes dull. *What is he saying?*

“I am saying that you should not smile at bastards like Crown Prince Detheus. It is irritating to feel like he and I are on the same level.”

Oh... That’s when I began to understand. He was thinking that because I acted the same way with Detheus as I did with him, he was being treated the same as that womanizing, complete moron, Detheus. *That’s not it at all.*

“You and Crown Prince Detheus are completely different,” I explained carefully.

“If that is so, then please treat us differently.”

What did I even do? I was trying not to look Detheus in the eye the whole time.

"It's a little strange, though."

Come to think of it, it was starting to sound like this was all my fault. As if it was my fault that the emperor was trying to set up Rodrigo with Delia again, my fault that I had smiled at the crown prince. *He's being ridiculous.*

"I'm sorry that you were annoyed. Actually, no. Why should I be apologizing for this? That's unfair." I was finally able to respond the way I wanted to.

Rodrigo shrugged. "You are right. It is not something you should apologize for, but I am irritated though. Why do you think that is?"

He responded with a question. We looked at each other and tilted our heads quizzically.

You're right, we're both acting a little weird today. What is this feeling?

"So, do you feel better now?"

In the distance, Kalen looked ready to throw a bomb at the carriage if we stayed any longer. His threatening aura was getting stronger. If Rodrigo was holding me here to try and aggravate Kalen, he had succeeded.

If Rodrigo wanted to sleep well tonight, we had to end it here for today. He said, "Come to think of it, I have been feeling better for a while now."

"Since when?"

"Since the princess was bombarded with hepao fruit, maybe?"

"Oh! That was so unfortunate," I feigned innocence. "She was dressed up all nicely and everything."

He chuckled. After checking on Kalen's location through the window, I turned to look at Rodrigo.

"Ahem, I should thank you properly. Thank you for rescuing your lover from danger." That was all he said before granting me a magnificent smile and exiting the carriage.

Did he realize I threw that rock? I was being sneaky. He's so perceptive. I wanted to know how he found out. But when I left the carriage to call Rodrigo, he had vanished without a trace.

It was extremely late. I was forced to listen to Ada and Ayla, who had just returned from their demon slaying, ranting about how they thought there was something suspicious going on between Rodrigo and the princess until just now.

"He's a womanizer!"

"He flirted with you even though he's already planning to marry Princess Delia. He's a scoundrel!"

According to them, Rodrigo was the worst man alive, but I had been the one to approach him first, and I had heard about what happened with Princess Delia. None of it was his fault.

Ada and Ayla remained persistent. In the end, I started dozing off while they ranted. Frustrated by this, they returned to their rooms. But once they were gone and I could lie down in bed, I was wide awake.

Maybe I should take a short walk.

I got out of bed and walked down the corridors. The fourth and fifth floors, where my immediate family members' bedrooms were, were not guarded. Only a couple of trustworthy servants stayed in small rooms attached to their masters' bedrooms, and the only people allowed to walk freely around the fourth and fifth floors of the Kartina manor were the Kartinas themselves. It was a nice, quiet place to take a walk when I needed to think.

As I wandered down the hall, I spotted a light shining from under Stefan's door at the end of the fourth-floor corridor.

Hm? Is dad still awake? He must be working late. I should tell him to go to bed earlier when I see him tomorrow.

I turned around so as not to disturb Stefan. And then, suddenly...

"What should we do about the assassins today, master?"

I heard a familiar voice.

CHAPTER FIFTEEN

The word "assassin" struck me. I stopped in my tracks and focused on the voices.

"Choose your best men."

"Will it really be all right?"

I recognized that voice. He was the leader of one of the Kartinas' secret organizations, the Shadow Gang. *Holland, was it?* I recalled the form of a burly man, very unlike the quiet voice.

"Hmph. If he can't even survive this, he's not good enough to court my Estella."

Good enough to court me? So, the assassins he's sending are going to the Erhart manor?

"Should I send them immediately?"

"Holland. There's no moon in the sky tonight. What did I tell you about this sort of day?"

"You said it was a good day to spill blood."

"Is there any reason for you to hesitate, then?" His voice was chilling.

"No. I will get them prepared and sent out immediately."

Shuffling and heavy footsteps; Holland about to take his leave. Before he departed, Stefan commanded that they should aim to succeed but that it would be fine if they simply scared him.

I returned to my room.

I knew what "succeeding" meant. Stefan was planning to kill Rodrigo. I had even shown him my tears, but Stefan seemed unable to acknowledge Rodrigo as my partner. Actually, he would react the same even if it wasn't Rodrigo.

I smiled bitterly, overwhelmed by Stefan's affection on the one hand and thankful on the other. If Rodrigo wasn't the ultimate victor of this ridiculous novel... if he wasn't the one who would massacre my family, I never would have gotten involved with him in the first place. But he was the male protagonist, and having watched him for a bit, it seemed like things wouldn't change much.

He was the perfect main character. I had to protect him and keep him alive, even if it looked like I was betraying my family, who loved me so dearly.

There's no time to waste.

Throwing off my pajamas, I snatched the black assassin garb from under my bed and put it on. The Shadow Gang of the Kartinas was cruel and showed no mercy. There was no way Rodrigo would die at their hands, but I was worried about the people at the Erhart manor. I couldn't let innocent people die because of Rodrigo. I couldn't let their deaths be my fault.

I took up my bow, shouldering my pouch full of poison bottles. Then I strapped a dagger to my thigh and put my hair in a bun.

What should I use to pin my hair?

As I considered this, the feather ornament that Stefan had given me for the banquet caught my eye. I took the ornament and stuck it in my hair, ready in record time.

I rang a small bell, causing Jane to appear at the door connecting my bedroom to hers. She must have been fast asleep because she staggered toward me with her eyes closed.

"Are you leaving again, my lady?" Jane asked, half asleep. "You said you wouldn't be going anywhere for a while."

Yeah, I really thought I wouldn't have to put on this outfit for a while.

I wasn't happy about this situation, either. "Things happened. I'll leave it to you, Jane."

"Be careful."

I had Jane lie in my bed, just in case. After pulling the blanket all the way up to her head, without hesitation, I jumped out the window.

Rodrigo, in the middle of reading reports, rubbed his tired eyes. There was too much to take care of. He was running several different businesses in various fields: mining, railroads, tourism, farming, and commerce.

None of them could be neglected, so whenever Rodrigo had the time, he took care of business himself. Rodrigo's secretary, Augus, had begged him to rest, but he was too anxious to do so. Whenever he was even a little careless, problems arose.

There had been a drug incident in his territory, a mine explosion, and recently, sand had been mixed into sacks of wheat being sold by his company. If natural disasters were the cause of these problems, he would have accepted the loss without question, but these disasters were manmade.

Sabotage, to be exact.

These were incidents designed to ruin Rodrigo. He was well aware of who it was that was targeting him, and of who was executing that person's orders. Starting to feel suffocated, as if something was constricting his chest, Rodrigo stretched and stood.

Tap. Tap. Tap.

Someone knocked on the window. *Who could it be at this time of night?* Rodrigo picked up the sword from beside his desk and hid next to the window. *Tap. Tap. Tap.* Little rocks pattered against the window again.

Rodrigo frowned and moved his hand. Immediately, all the lights in his room went out. Carefully, he drew open the window. A black figure entered his office. Without hesitating, Rodrigo swung his sword. *Clang!* Metal clashed with metal.

"Ahhh, stop it, Rodrigo. I-it's me, Estella!"

Rodrigo, who was about to attack again, paused at the sound of the panicked voice. "Estella?"

The voice was familiar. He snapped his fingers, and a small candle lit up. The yellow flickering light fell on a figure that was rather short for an assassin. The figure hooked a finger over a dark mask, lowering it.

"It's me."

Ha! Rodrigo let out a breath in exasperation. It really was Estella.

"I thought I was going to die. How could you just swing your sword at me like that without warning?"

"I thought you were an assassin." Rodrigo barely looked at the grumbling Estella and went over to sit on the couch. "Why are you here?"

"For a rescue mission." Estella smiled brightly as she stepped closer to him. He looked at her as if she was being ridiculous.

"Whoever wants to court you really needs a sturdy heart, Estella. I almost died from shock. Have you heard of heart attacks?"

"Hm, I asked you out because I thought you were sturdy. Technically, I proposed to you." Estella nonchalantly brushed off his complaints.

"I'm in top shape today. And I'm perfectly capable of taking care of assa—"

"Arghhh!"

Rodrigo was about to turn Estella away when they heard a scream from somewhere downstairs. Rodrigo sprang to his feet. Estella pulled her mask back up.

She quickly whispered, "I'm not here to rescue you. There's no time, so let's talk later."

Estella rushed out of the room.

"Ah... Ahhh!"

The screaming sounded from the entrance of the manor. The members of the Shadow Gang were unleashing their attacks on the Erharts' knights. I slid down the banister to get downstairs faster.

Please, please, let me save at least one!

But unfortunately, when I got to the lobby, the knights who had been on guard duty were all on the floor. Shadows flickered along the walls and ceiling. The Shadow Gang was disappearing into the darkness. The throats that had just been screaming had been slit.

I removed the finger I had placed under the nose of a fallen knight to check his breathing and closed my eyes. The Shadow Gang could not be tracked by sight.

They lived off the darkness. Some said that they had been raised on the blood of demons, and others said that they were the spawn of witches. To track their swift movements, you had to chase their subtle scent.

Swish.

Someone approached me. I waited patiently until he was close enough. And as soon as the scent of the Shadow Gang grew stronger, I reached behind me without looking and stabbed the figure with a needle I had hidden in my palm. Before the man could even choke out a cry, he clutched his neck and collapsed. This caused a stir among the Shadow Gang.

Sorry. You're not dead, though.

I prayed that the Shadow Gang would leave of their own accord. But my wish was not granted. The Shadow Gang seemed to have decided to ignore me—they moved toward Rodrigo's room.

They're really focused on their mission.

And then more knights came spilling onto the scene.

"Assassins have gotten in! Search everywhere!"

Things got more complicated. I needed to keep my identity hidden from both the Shadow Gang and Rodrigo's knights. I ducked behind a pillar. If the Erhart knights saw me, dressed in all black, they'd certainly mistake me for an assassin.

And if the Shadow Gang found me, they'd try to kill me, thinking I was just one of Rodrigo's knights. *What do I do? This is bad.*

As I contemplated this, I could sense the Shadow Gang moving above my head. They climbed the chandeliers and the walls like spiders. This wasn't the time to worry about my own safety.

Rodrigo!

"Commander, there's an unconscious assassin here!"

The Erhart knights charged over to where the assassin lay.

Now!

In two leaps, I landed on the stairs. Thankfully, no one noticed. As soon as I felt a sense of relief, a dagger slashed toward my head.

The Shadow Gang! Those bastards!

I rolled out of the way at the sudden attack. The loud sounds I made were unavoidable.

"It's the assassin!"

It was obvious that I would be noticed.

"Ugh, this is too much!"

I ran up the stairs faster than anyone. Since I was chasing the Shadow Gang, our destination was the same. The Erharts' knights chased after me. A deadly race through the halls in the middle of the night.

"I have to get out there."

"You may not."

"I can take care of myself."

"I know, but you may not leave."

Rodrigo resented himself for not stopping Estella. He didn't expect Gunther to enter the room as soon as she left.

Gunther had advised Rodrigo to stay inside the room because assassins had entered the manor and it was dangerous to leave. "If you want to leave, you'll have to cut me down first."

Gunther tilted his head, revealing his neck. The sounds of a bloody battle erupted outside. Screams and hurried footsteps. Estella was out there with her promises to protect him. *No, she said she wasn't here to protect me today, but someone else.*

In any case, she was going against the Kartinas to protect the Erharts. It made no sense for him, the family head, to wait inside the room.

"A-a-are you really going to cut me down?" Gunther stuttered in panic as Rodrigo adjusted his grip on his sword.

"No, I'm going to knock you out." Rodrigo swung his sword, still inside its scabbard, and Gunther left the door unguarded for a moment as he ducked out of the way. That brief moment was the problem. With a loud bang, the door was thrown open and a horde of black-clad assassins crowded into the room.

They slashed at Rodrigo. Despite the sudden attack, Rodrigo blocked every blade with his own without missing a beat. He also didn't forget to put some distance between them and himself by backing up. The Erhart knights ran into the room soon after. The office wasn't small, but with twenty strong men crowding around him, it felt cramped.

A bloody battle ensued. The assassins cut down anyone in their way, left and right. The Erhart knights fought by the book, but the assassins fought dirty. Naturally, the odds were in the assassins' favor. But there was someone who could turn the tide.

Rodrigo.

He gripped his sword and jumped into the fray. Amidst the dozens of swords tangled up in the crowded space, his ability to exploit any opening he saw by stabbing and then backing away again was excellent.

"Gunther, back!" Rodrigo shouted for Gunther to guard his back. In the meantime, most of the knights had collapsed, and two of the assassins were coughing up blood.

Those damned Kartinas.

Rodrigo ground his teeth. At that moment, a not-at-all welcome voice rang out from the window.

"What is all this?" It was Estella, her clear voice juxtaposing the bloody sounds of battle.

CHAPTER
SIXTEEN

Hot on their heels, I pretended to follow the Shadow Gang up the stairs, before throwing myself out of an open window. I made my way up to Rodrigo's room by climbing the wall outside. I nearly had to scale the walls barehanded, but thankfully, I had brought a thin but sturdy Kartina-made rope with me.

It meant that I would be spared Jane's lecture on what I had done to my hands. My plan had been to meet up with Rodrigo, calmly explain the situation, and send the Erhart knights away first. Then, with Rodrigo's help, I would have fought back against the Shadow Gang.

I had everything planned out. But the chaotic scene I was faced with left no room for my plans. There was no way I could explain anything with all these people fighting to the death in this cramped space. I urgently opened my mouth at the sight of the battlefield that would only cease with the complete annihilation of one side.

"Can't you see?"

A sword was thrust toward Rodrigo, who had approached me. Rodrigo, who had turned to dodge the attack instinctively, paused.

Why isn't he dodging?

"Get out of here!" Rodrigo yelled, pushing his attacker away with sheer force.

"Why?" I ignored Rodrigo's warning and lightly jumped into the office. I shouted, "I'll take care of this. Just cover your mouth."

Everyone was going to die at this rate. *I guess I'm the only one who can put a stop to this right now.* I emptied the contents of my bag onto the floor. The glass bottles from my bag broke on impact, and smoke filled the room.

Clang! Clang!

In the thick of the smoke, I heard the sound of swords hitting the floor. Soon, large bodies also toppled down.

"Ugh. What is this?"

"Oh? Did you not cover your mouth?" I quickly placed a chair behind Rodrigo as he collapsed. Thanks to me, he was able to sit on the chair instead of falling to the ground. Then I quickly climbed onto his lap and pressed my hands over his mouth.

"It's a narcotic, a very powerful one."

Rodrigo groggily closed and opened his eyes, muttering, "I don't know if I should be happy about your skills or worried about how reckless you are."

I could feel his lips tickling my palm with every word he said. It created strange sensations, so I pressed my hands against him even harder. "Be quiet. I can't take care of all this by myself. You cannot fall asleep."

I made sure to emphasize that. Rodrigo nodded. Soon, the thick smoke dissipated, trickling out the open window after doing its job, and I could see the gruesome scene.

Pulling my hands from Rodrigo's mouth, I climbed off his lap, unable to hold back a sigh. Rodrigo shook his head from side to side before looking up at me.

"Why are you looking at me like that?" I muttered, embarrassed by the way he stared at me.

"Why are you looking at me like that?" Estella asked.

Yeah. Why am I staring at you?

Her mask had slipped down a little to reveal the drops of sweat clinging to her forehead.

Is this just out of curiosity? Why are you trying so hard?

He took some time to look at Estella. Despite the time they had spent together, he had never looked at her very closely.

Her lovely features and fair skin suited her flushed cheeks and crimson lips. Her beauty could easily turn heads, gentle and pure, and it was hard to imagine her being adept at poisons, swinging a sword, or throwing shuriken.

Maybe she's not a Kartina.

It was a wistful hope. But then Rodrigo shook his head. She was a Kartina. And not just any Kartina, but the Kartina family's cherished treasure. That meant that he had to keep his interest in her in check.

Rodrigo responded gruffly, "This has gone too far, so someone must take responsibility. The Erharts will demand compensation from the Kartinas. Is that clear?"

Estella slowly turned her head and met his gaze. Her expression made Rodrigo's insides tighten. *How will she respond? Did I offend her?*

Rodrigo was eager to hear her answer. There really wasn't much he could do. It wasn't like the Kartinas would respond to the Erharts' demands. If he sent someone to collect compensation for damages, the messenger would be lucky to get out alive. But Rodrigo wanted to see how Estella would react.

How will she react to a demand that will clearly put her family at a disadvantage?

If she became angry or defensive, he wouldn't be able to trust her promise to protect him from the Kartinas. Rodrigo stared deeply into Estella's eyes, clear as the sky. She frowned, contemplative.

I guess she is a Kartina after all. His chest felt tight. He wanted to open the windows and get some fresh air. *I shouldn't have asked.* Rodrigo regretted his words.

What? Regret?

Surprise jolted through him. He was not familiar with regret. Estella was like a pebble thrown into a lake. She had jumped in and sunk into his life against his wishes.

"Does it worry you? That I might demand too much from the Kartinas?"

Estella shook her head. The impulse to brush away the strands of hair sticking to her face made Rodrigo's hand twitch. Absently, he reached toward her, but Estella was quicker. She removed the feather ornament from her hair, stuck it between her lips, and gathered and pinned her hair up into a bun. Even those small movements affected him greatly.

Damn it, what's wrong with me? Rodrigo furrowed his eyebrows and scowled.

"Are you that angry?" Estella asked. "I'm sorry for failing to stop them properly."

It was commonplace for the Kartinas to send assassins. He had known about the Shadow Gang as well. There was no reason for her to feel guilty. There may have been more assassins this time, but for the Kartinas and the Erharts, a few assassins were no big deal.

"Go ahead and make your demands, Rodrigo."

Rodrigo raised his eyebrows.

"Demand that they pay for a grand funeral for your fallen knights and take responsibility for their families. Let's see what else you could demand." The reason Estella had taken some time to respond to Rodrigo was because she had been thinking about compensation for the Erharts. The Kartinas had more than enough money. If money were enough to assuage Rodrigo, if his resentment toward the Kartinas could be resolved even a little through financial compensation, it would be a profitable deal for them.

Estella was willing to grant Rodrigo anything, short of killing one of her family members. To be more precise, she was willing to convince her parents to give into whatever Rodrigo demanded.

"Huh? Do you even know what you're saying?" His suspicion toward Estella was swept away like sand with the receding tide. The tension in Rodrigo's body subsided. He casually sat on the windowsill and looked at Estella.

"I said I'd compensate you."

"I am asking whether you know what that means."

Estella smiled faintly. "Of course, I do."

"Your family's reputation would hit rock bottom."

Did the Kartinas even have a reputation to uphold? Everyone bowed down to the Kartinas in public before turning around and badmouthing them behind their backs.

And then they would turn to the Kartinas to do their dirty work.

"That's not important."

"Your family's reputation is not important?" Rodrigo tipped his head. Reputation was a matter of life and death for nobles. They were the kind of people who secretly committed all kinds of misdeeds but were terrified of scandals. Then again, if they were concerned with their reputation, they wouldn't commit so many evil deeds.

The Mave Guild. Everyone knew the Kartinas were behind this information-gathering agency that also undertook missions, committed all sorts of evil acts, and supposedly did anything for money.

"Come, now that you've brought it up, let's think of what else you should be compensated for. We're richer than you think." Estella patted the couch seat beside her. Ironically, she looked elegant and even dignified, sitting on a couch covered in blood.

It doesn't suit her at all. Rodrigo ran his hand through his disheveled hair and sat down next to Estella. He said, "Is that so? Good. Then I should go all out. I want to take away the Kartinas' most cherished treasure."

For a moment, there was a strange glint in Rodrigo's eyes. They then fell silent. Listening to the even breathing of the unconscious men, they simply wrote up an extensive list of demands.

"Rodrigo."

Rodrigo and I wrote up a simple request for compensation with a list of items. Near the fallen assassins, I called him back over to me, to tell him something about the Shadow Gang. He put the request in an envelope that wasn't splattered with blood and turned to look at me.

"This is the Shadow Gang's token. You know that the Shadow Gang is a secret organization under the direct control of my family, right?" I stuck my hand down one of the assassins' pants.

"What do you think you're doing?" Rodrigo's eyes widened, and he darted across the room to me, yanking my hand away.

What does he think I'm doing?

I narrowed my eyes and looked at him. Then I dangled a small incense pouch in front of him. "Hm? I was just taking out the Shadow Gang's token."

"That does not mean you should stick your hand down a man's pants. If he was awake, you could go straight to jail. Are you aware of that?"

"He's asleep anyway. The narcotic I make is really effective. You could carry him off and he wouldn't know. You could probably teleport him with magic, and he still wouldn't wake up."

And the pouch was technically hidden by the side of his hips. *I'm not a pervert, you know.*

I raised both of my hands in protest. Then I handed Rodrigo the incense pouch, asking, "Can you smell it?"

There was no way he couldn't. The pouch emitted a subtle scent that was not overwhelming, but not exactly desirable, either. Rodrigo backed away. I held the pouch out farther toward him.

"This scent distracts people. Those who aren't feeling well or tend to have a lot on their minds show momentary symptoms of blurry vision or brain fog if they're exposed to even just a whiff of this scent," I continued. "It also has a relaxing effect. That's how they distract the guards."

"Is that why the Shadow Gang seems to be almost supernaturally elusive?"

"That's right. Nobody thinks that it might be due to these incense pouches."

"Is there an antidote?" he asked.

"It's not a poison, so no. You just have to build up a tolerance for it. I'll get you more, so just increase the amount in small doses. You get what I mean, right?"

Rodrigo nodded, but then his gaze darkened. "Is there a reason you are revealing this family secret to me?"

Sometimes, when he got serious like this, my heart would sink. I pressed my lips together and met his stare. We searched each other's eyes, looking for something...

I was the first one to turn away. My eyelashes trembled. Rodrigo grabbed at his cravat and loosened it, seemingly irritated.

Do you want to know why I'm telling you everything? In order to survive, it would have been better to tell some reasonable lies and hatch an escape plan. But that's not what I did. *Because I...*

"Because I trust you."

Rodrigo's hand paused. Something in him seemed to have snapped.

CHAPTER
SEVENTEEN

Tap. Tap. Tap.

Devlon was unable to focus due to the repetitive sound.

"Your Grace! Please let me work!" Devlon ended up committing the transgression of yelling at his master.

"Go ahead, who's stopping you?" Rodrigo answered dismissively before moving his legs off his desk. He stared at the incense pouch sitting on his desk.

"Come to the manor with the compensation request today." Estella's voice echoed in his mind.

"Is that something important? Are you aware that you have been staring at it all morning? If you do not have any work to do, you could help me," Devlon grumbled.

Numerous reports on the knights who passed away last night were piled on his desk. Rodrigo had ordered Devlon to finish compiling a list of related compensation expenses by that afternoon.

Today must be jinxed.

Devlon sighed. As soon as he had shown up for work that morning, things had been disconcerting. A corner of the office had been taken up by a pile of bodies, the smell of blood and steel filling the room.

He grimaced automatically thinking of that morning when he had let out a yell, thinking they were all dead. At first, he thought they *were* all dead.

"They're just asleep."

Rodrigo's voice had been kind, but his ensuing explanation was sparse. It had been Devlon's job to take care of everything. He had to slap the knights awake and send them home, identify the fallen knights, and the Shadow Gang...

"Can we kill them now?"

"Let them be, they're awake."

One of the assassins' fingers had twitched. As soon as Rodrigo and Devlon were distracted, the Shadow Gang disappeared. Technically, they had given them a chance to escape, as the two had been well aware of their movements.

And then the work began.

"I'm taking it to the Kartinas. Make sure that your calculations are correct."

"The Kartinas?" Devlon dropped the fountain pen he was holding.

"What?"

"I thought you were dating one of the daughters?"

"I am."

"And you quite liked her."

Rodrigo, who hated anything troublesome, had not only gone to visit the Kartina manor himself, but the day before, he had joined the Kartinas on their way home from the palace in the crown prince's carriage, which he wouldn't usually go near. And the numerous stories about them in the newspapers hadn't fazed him at all.

In the past, Rodrigo would prevent any and all gossip about him from being published by buying up the newspaper companies or starting his own newspaper and publishing an even bigger story. Ultimately, the only explanation for his changed behavior was that Rodrigo quite liked Estella. *A reasonable deduction.*

"Is it that obvious?"

Devlon was taken aback by Rodrigo's deadpan reply. *Did he just admit his feelings for Lady Estella?*

"W-w-wait! But you still want to demand that her family pay for the damages? The family of the lady you like?"

"Is that not allowed?"

"Of course not!"

Rodrigo agreed with Devlon on this. *But she said I should. Herself. And she said I should go all out.*

"Shouldn't you want to shower her with gifts if you like her? I'm not saying you should send the Kartinas any gifts. Because if you do, I will be leaving your service without hesitation. Anyway, isn't it unnecessary to add fuel to the fire when your two families are already on bad terms?"

Rodrigo rested his chin on his hand and eyed Devlon.

"Wh-what is it?"

Rodrigo's lips spread into a smile. But his narrowed eyes were almost piercingly cold.

"Are you interested in Lady Estella?"

As if! Devlon shook his head. It wasn't even winter, but there was a chill in the air. Devlon wrapped his arms around himself and rubbed his biceps. *A Kartina? Even if I had dozens of them to choose from. Never!*

"Augus, did you prepare what I asked for?" Rodrigo prompted.

He was almost ready to head out. After fastening the cufflinks handed to him by his servant, he stood in front of the mirror. The black suit embroidered with gold suited him quite well. The new custom suit he bought because Augus insisted that he stop wearing his tattered suit fit him perfectly. It emphasized his wide shoulders and strong physique. *I didn't think I needed it, but I'm glad I had it made.*

"Everything is ready. These are the documents."

Rodrigo paged through the heap of papers handed to him by Augus and nodded. He seemed satisfied, and Augus smiled at this.

"What are you planning to do with these?"

"Devlon told me that it's common sense to shower the person you like with gifts. So, I'm going to charm my lover."

Augus blinked. *Did I hear that right?* But Rodrigo seemed completely serious, so he must have heard correctly. Augus' jaw dropped in a belated reaction. He never imagined that Rodrigo would say something like this. He tried, "I must have heard wrong. Would you please repeat that, Your Grace?"

Rodrigo's crimson lips spread into a pleasant smile. "I said I would be stealing the Kartina treasure."

Rodrigo laughed merrily. It took Augus a while to understand what he meant by "the Kartina treasure." Even after Rodrigo had adjusted his cufflinks once more and perfectly tied his cravat, Augus still had no idea. When he finally realized that Rodrigo was referring to a Kartina, and that he was planning on charming a Kartina, Augus groaned.

Rodrigo had never before made any sort of effort to gain someone's affection. Everyone, excluding the emperor and the Kartinas, fell for him without any effort on his part. Though many kept their distance from him because of the

Kartinas' evildoings targeting him, in general, everyone viewed him positively.

Especially women.

There were thousands of women who sent long-winded love letters that Augus was forced to reject with individual replies on behalf of Rodrigo. Just a single glance was all it took to make women clutch their hearts and faint, and a mere gesture was enough to make someone's nose bleed. Augus had repeatedly witnessed such strange phenomena. It would only be natural for someone getting that much attention from women to find at least one of them interesting, but Rodrigo was practically a statue.

His disinterest was so absolute that there had been a rumor circulating among the ladies who had fallen for him that he, in fact, liked men instead of women.

The many magazine companies they had bought up to stop this gossip from spreading were still in the Erharts' possession. Now, this man just announced that he not only liked Estella, but that he would be trying to actively win her over.

No, he said he would steal her. What does that mean? Could he really be in love? No way...

The Rodrigo that Augus served was not someone you would associate with something as sweet as love. His life had been too tragic, his rise from rock bottom too arduous, and that had left him with too many flaws to dream of romance. Rodrigo needed a woman who grew up in a loving family and was able to embrace his flaws like a warm light.

But a Kartina, of all people?

Augus felt his mouth dry up as if it were filled with sand. He was starting to worry about his master.

"What? Who?"

With a crack, the neck of the monster in Stefan's grasp snapped. The broken neckbone of the monster pierced its skin, and green blood trickled down Stefan's hand.

"Sir Rodrigo Erhart is here."

Lanst, the Kartinas' butler, fixed his gaze on his master's shoes, which were splattered with blood, and waited for Stefan to respond. Stefan tossed the monster's corpse aside and scattered some food that attracts monsters around him. Having smelled the animal's blood, more of the beasts came running toward them on all fours through the trees.

Stefan drew his sword and cut them down without hesitation.

Splat!

Their blood sprayed over the ground like rain, pooling. Lanst immediately realized that Stefan was in a bad mood, but could only bow his head further, knowing that he couldn't do anything about it.

"Let's go deal with that damn bastard."

"Will you be going like this?" Thinking he should evacuate the newer Kartina servants, Lanst inquired after Stefan's wishes.

They were behind the Kartina manor on Kartina property. The mountains behind the manor had been turned into a giant labyrinth filled with monsters, making it a monster hunting ground for Stefan to relieve his stress and for the young Kartinas and Kartina soldiers to train in. Killing was necessary here. Naturally, his clothes and sword had been dirtied and soaked in green blood.

Stefan might have been ill-tempered, but he kept himself clean. Unlike his brothers, who were more on the burly side, Stefan was a handsome man with a lithe physique. Many a person had fallen for that face and into ruin as a result. He was well aware of the fact that he was rather handsome, and so whenever he met anyone, he made sure to make himself presentable, which meant being clean and well-dressed, though not always extravagantly.

But Stefan was planning to show up covered in blood. This meant that he didn't consider Rodrigo to be worth even common courtesy. Lanst felt a headache coming on. He was aware of the reason for the gloomy atmosphere around the manor these past few days. The servants were all aflutter.

The youngest lady's fateful love.

All kinds of ridiculous rumors were circulating, saying that the Kartinas' cherished youngest daughter had been seduced by the devil, or that their tragic love might resolve the animosity between the Kartinas and the Erharts. The servants' deep interest in this issue was directly proportional to their loyalty toward their masters.

Lanst was sympathetic to the gossip that arose from their loyalty, but he did not participate in it. Instead, he reprimanded his subordinates and kept his mouth shut. In all honesty, he had no interest in the lady's love life.

He simply wished for the manor to be quiet and peaceful, that all misdeeds would be carried out far away from the manor, and that this place would remain peaceful. It was a humble wish from the Kartinas' elderly butler who had served them for three generations.

By the time Rodrigo reached the Kartina reception room, he had gone through a lot.

Why do they have so many traps in their manor?

He had managed to avoid two separate spike traps that shot out from the floor, managed to block ten arrows, and discovered twenty snares. The whole house was practically a trap.

This place would be safe even if a war broke out. Rodrigo took note of the more effective traps and contemplated implementing them at the Erhart manor.

"Lady Estella has arrived."

Finally, the woman he was here to charm. Rodrigo stood and adjusted his suit.

I realized Rodrigo was here when the sound of explosions reached my ears.

"Sir Rodrigo is here," Jane confirmed after returning from assessing the situation outside.

"I see, he's early."

"Did you know he was coming?" Jane asked.

I grinned in lieu of a reply. I asked, "How long do you think it'll take him? To get here."

"I'm not sure. It should take him at least an hour."

It was enough time to get changed. Realizing my intention, Jane quickly brought out a dress.

"You must really like Sir Rodrigo, my lady. If you're getting changed for him."

"I wouldn't date him if I didn't." I felt bad about having to keep Jane, my best friend, in the dark, but I had no choice. After all, to deceive your enemies, you must first deceive your allies.

"You're all done."

Jane was quick. I was ready much sooner than I had expected. I looked at myself in the mirror. A beautiful face looked back at me.

Ha... how pretty.

I admired my beauty once more as I got up.

"Let's go."

I was looking forward to his list of demands and how he would present it. I walked down to the reception room with light footsteps.

CHAPTER
EIGHTEEN

"You're here early, Rodrigo."

Rodrigo, who had risen from his seat, looked sleek but dazzling in his black suit. You could dress him in rags, and he would still look stunning thanks to his handsome face.

"You look beautiful," he said, a simple compliment.

"Try to put some more effort into that compliment."

He chuckled at my words, pausing thoughtfully. Then he said, "You remind me of a green meadow in summer. A rose brooch would be perfect…"

I asked for a compliment and he's waxing poetic.

"Augus," Rodrigo called the man beside him.

His butler, I think?

"Yes, Your Grace."

"The ruby mine in the western Rubiste region."

"Yes?"

"Transfer the ownership. By tomorrow."

"The paperwork is quite complicated. It would take at least a week."

"Hm."

Rodrigo grunted in dissatisfaction. While I was in the middle of giving orders to the servants next to me, I could feel his gaze on me. I also heard him tapping on the desk. When I turned back to them, Augus looked flustered.

"I will hound the administrative officers and reduce the wait to four days," he said.

"You've got three days."

"Three days, understood. But who do you want me to transfer ownership of the ruby mine to?"

"Estella."

"What?" It wasn't Augus who had responded this time, but me. Augus was calmly writing down his orders in a notebook. "What did you say, Rodrigo?"

"I said I'd transfer ownership of my ruby mine to you." Rodrigo used casual speech, mindful of the Kartina manor servants in the room.

"Why?" I asked, but immediately stuck my hand out toward his mouth. "Actually," I continued, "don't answer that. Let me guess."

He suddenly wanted to give me a ruby mine. *Why would he do that?* Rodrigo watched me carefully, arms crossed over his chest.

"Oh, I know!" The answer was obvious. I walked around the long desk and stopped beside Rodrigo. I leaned toward him so that the others couldn't hear, my golden hair spilling over my shoulder and brushing Rodrigo's cheek. It must have tickled him because he flinched.

"You want to make sure the Kartinas don't interfere with your business operations, right? If it's under my name, they would leave it alone. All right, go ahead and use me as much as you need to. I'm fine with it. And don't worry, I'll return it all to you later."

Rodrigo let out a short sigh.

Ha! I solved his little riddle. I went to sit down across from him, incredibly pleased with myself. Maybe it was because I had figured it out so quickly, but Rodrigo didn't look happy.

"Estella, you seem to have misunderstood, but this gift is purely—"

Bang! The door went flying. Snapped from its hinges, it came swinging toward Rodrigo's neck. Rodrigo scowled and shot up from his seat.

Crash! The door shattered a window.

"I must have underestimated my strength because I've been out slaughtering monsters. Are you all right, Your Grace?"

It was Stefan. Green blood trickled down his silver hair. He looked dreadful, glaring at Rodrigo as if ready to kill him.

The way he stood in the now permanently open doorway was akin to a hellhound guarding the gates of the underworld.

"Dad!" I immediately took out a handkerchief and ran over to him. As I wiped his messy face, Stefan's mood seemed to soften. The massive change honestly surprised me as well. It was like suddenly switching genres from a hardcore, R-rated male-reader oriented novel to a rosy romantic fantasy involving parenting.

"Dad, were you out hunting monsters? But you went to bed late again last night and got up early this morning." I began to nag, sounding worried about him. He liked it when I nagged him. The Kartinas had no interest in each other, though I was an exception. The relationship between Hela, my mom, and Stefan wasn't bad, but she never nagged him.

They barely ever spoke, really.

Maybe that was why Stefan took my nagging as a sign of affection. He roared with laughter, wiping his hand on a relatively clean spot on his clothes, and patted my head.

"How sweet of you, my darling daughter," he said.

I sighed inwardly as I watched Lanst, who stood behind Stefan, dabbing at his teary eyes with a handkerchief. I felt sorry for Lanst. *Is it normal for a butler to be so moved by such trivial moments of peace in the manor?*

I heard Rodrigo approach from behind as Lanst's face grew pale. It seemed he knew what might happen should Rodrigo and Stefan clash. Poor Lanst.

But what can you do? This is the only way we can all survive.

"It has been a while, Sir Stefan. I am here to settle a bill, but if you need time to get ready, I shall wait here while having tea with Estella."

Stefan stepped back as if unwilling to look up at Rodrigo, who was a bit taller than him. Then he pulled me aside, so I wasn't standing between them.

"You are unnecessarily tall, Your Grace," he growled. "And you want to have tea with Estella, just the two of you?"

Stefan's frightening tone made it clear that he was ready to funnel poison into Rodrigo's mouth. Then, Stefan threatened to paralyze his tongue if he kept spouting nonsense. "Go ahead and say whatever you like while your tongue still functions."

Ugh, my head hurts.

Stefan's eyes glinted with malice. He wiped away the monster blood trickling down his cheek with the back of his hand as he glared at Rodrigo. "Let's settle that bill now."

Stefan and Rodrigo sat down together. I drifted between the seat next to Stefan and the seat next to Rodrigo—but ultimately decided to sit next to Stefan.

I'm still a Kartina, after all. And it seems like Rodrigo can keep his cool, but my dad can't.

"I shall get straight to the point."

"Why not have a cup of tea first?" Stefan pushed a cup full of warm tea that Lanst had poured toward Rodrigo. He openly dipped his bloody fingers into the tea while doing so.

"Oh, excuse me!"

There was no apology. He didn't offer a different teacup, either. Depending on the type of monster, monster blood could be poisonous or medicinal. The neon green blood Stefan had just mixed into the tea was that of a spider monster, which could blur your vision and often worse.

I contemplated pulling at the tablecloth, feigning ignorance, but ultimately decided against it.

"Oh no, I spilled the tea." Rodrigo took his teacup and dropped it onto the ground.

It looked like an honest mistake, but the problem was his tone...

Just as expected, when he realized Rodrigo had dropped his teacup on purpose, Stefan began to seethe with murderous intent. The reception room felt so cold that I was surprised ice crystals weren't forming in the air.

"Dad, you promised me you would be my dance partner for my dance lesson today. The teacher should be here soon," I tried to add some warmth.

It was a strength training session disguised as a dance lesson. Stefan's fury extinguished like a flame doused in water. I patted his arm but still kept feeling Rodrigo's gaze on me.

Why are you staring at me? When I turned slightly to glance at him, I met his red eyes. Something in my heart stirred. I pursed my lips and frowned at him. *Just tell him what you need to and hurry home.*

At my meaningful look, Rodrigo held out the documents.

"Assassins invaded last night."

I sat up straight, pulling my hands away from Stefan. I was curious to see how he would react.

"Oh? It looks like we're not the only ones who hate the Erharts." Stefan slyly feigned innocence.

"They were Kartina assassins." Rodrigo held out the Shadow Gang incense pouch. Stefan faltered. Rodrigo might not have noticed, but sitting next to him, I could tell.

He must be curious as to how Rodrigo discovered the incense pouch. The Shadow Gang assassins kept them well hidden in their clothes. Rodrigo would have had to strip them all down and search through their belongings to find the pouches. But even then, the pouches were made to look like part of their clothes, so they were still hard to find.

Unless someone had told him where to look. Stefan would never even dream that I was that very someone. *I'm sorry, dad.*

"If you need evidence, I have plenty. Do you need more?"

Stefan furrowed his eyebrows at Rodrigo's firm words. After all, his confidence meant that there was reliable evidence. It was easy to explain away the incense pouch and say it had nothing to do with us, but it would be a different story if Rodrigo had more evidence to show.

Stefan glanced at me. Maybe he remembered my plea to stop tormenting Rodrigo. Drawing back a bit, he said, "Let's say they were ours. I never ordered them to do anything. This seems to be a personal vendetta."

"Personal vendetta or not, it does not matter. We have lost some of our cherished knights, and the families of those knights have lost husbands and fathers."

My heart twinged painfully. That was why I had gone there last night despite the danger... but my efforts had been insufficient. I always knew the Kartinas did evil things, but seeing the victim—and in the end, Rodrigo was the master of those victims, and would be the one responsible for taking care of them—my heart ached.

"What do you want?"

"Normally, this would warrant the following amount of compensation."

A thick report dropped heavily onto the desk. It seemed to consist of supplementary documents for the list of items we had written up yesterday.

Wow, he must have been up all night. Come to think of it, Rodrigo did look a bit tired.

"The price of some insignificant knight's life is an entire gold bar?" The corner of Stefan's lips formed into a smirk.

"The price? Can you set a price on a person's life? This is to compensate for the time they should have had left to live."

Stefan sneered at Rodrigo's words. Rodrigo was definitely not the type of person Stefan liked. Stefan was a utilitarian. And by that, I mean that he was selfish.

He did not value people's lives. He believed that the worth of a life was determined by rank. Even if they died together on the battlefield, it mattered whether the person was a general, a soldier, or just a pack mule. Anyone below the rank of soldier would not even have their corpse retrieved.

In other words, to Stefan, Rodrigo must have looked like an incredibly inefficient and idealistic brat.

Stefan placed his chin on his hand, as if to prompt him to keep going. Rodrigo frowned.

"In total, that will be fifty gold bars."

"What? My boys managed to kill fifty knights? I should throw them a party." He was flustered. Fifty gold bars might not be a significant amount to Stefan, but it wasn't the kind of money he could just easily acquire either.

"But I will not be demanding that amount." Rodrigo said curtly, and Stefan narrowed his eyes. "Fifty gold bars is far too cheap. This incident could very well turn into a war between our families."

Stefan tensed, ready to fight. But that fighting spirit would soon evaporate, to be replaced with fury.

"The Erharts will cover the knights' compensation. In return, allow me to take Estella out on a date."

"How dare you?!" Stefan slammed his fists onto the desk.

"We are talking about fifty gold bars. And I will forget about all of the atrocities the Kartinas have committed toward the Erharts as well."

"Ha! Why don't you just ask for a war? I will pretend this conversation never happened. Come on, Estella." He stood and extended his hand toward me. "That bastard must be insane. He thinks a measly fifty gold bars is enough for a date with you!"

Huh... why?

CHAPTER
NINETEEN

Why is he holding out his hand in the middle of his conversation with Rodrigo? What could it mean? Does he want me to hold it?

I stared at Stefan's outstretched hand. His gaze shook violently.

"E-Estella... take my hand and let's go." Stefan's tone was desperate.

He wants me to turn the tables and leave with him. I looked at Rodrigo. It was impossible to tell what he was thinking as he politely sat there. Stefan, on the other hand, almost twitched with anxiety and restlessness.

"Estella, that amount is nothing. We're rich, Estella. We even have a gold mine in the south."

Does he think I'm worried about our financial situation? That's not it at all. I was tempted solely by Rodrigo's offer to forget all the atrocities the Kartinas had committed so far.

That would give us a clean slate, right? In that case, a few dates would be fine. We're supposed to be dating anyway.

"Dad."

"Estella, please..." Stefan looked at me like a puppy left in the rain.

Sorry, dad, but I've already decided.

"All right." I accepted Rodrigo's offer.

Rumble... Storm clouds filled the reception room, followed by thunder and lightning. Above Stefan's head, that is.

"Since this concerns me, I would like to make this decision."

It was sad that Rodrigo and I had to barter like this just for a date. But the saddest person right now was Stefan. His expression made that very clear. I winced when I saw how distraught he was.

The servants gulped and eyed Stefan anxiously. He was a powder keg that could go off at any moment. There were plenty of lethal weapons within his reach.

To avoid any tragic incidents, those entering the reception room left their weapons outside, out of principle. But what did it matter? My dad was capable of cutting someone's throat with just a plate.

I looked over at the servants, hoping that the newly purchased, luxurious carpet would not be drenched in blood.

I'm sorry.

"Estella, you know this isn't just because of the compensation, right? Since your father would never allow me to take you out on a date, I had no choice. I don't want you to have to deceive your parents to meet up with me."

Is this what you call a wolf in sheep's clothing? I was willing to bet my entire fortune that Rodrigo was enjoying himself right now. *He's not quite sane, either.*

He smiled nonchalantly and leaned back in his chair.

Boom!

Stefan slammed his fist down onto the marble-top table. The marble cracked clean in half with the strike. As always, their meeting came to a close with a great financial loss.

"Estella, it's not too late."

Stefan followed me around, trying to change my mind. It was part of a long series of attempts at persuading me to change my mind that had started the moment I accepted Rodrigo's offer and gone on throughout my training lesson.

"What a shameless bastard. Small misunderstandings and quarrels break out between families all the time, you know. But he's using that to blackmail us!"

The problem was that it wasn't just small misunderstandings and quarrels. It wasn't simply a matter of spreading false rumors, getting snubbed at a banquet, or political isolation. The Kartinas had purposefully ruined Rodrigo's mining business by mixing impurities into his iron ore, causing him to suffer those losses directly.

The Kartinas secretly financed newspapers that printed malicious slander about the Erharts, and whenever Rodrigo purchased a building, they would buy the one next to it and compete with his business. They had yet to mess with Rodrigo's people directly, but if I didn't stop them, they were the kind of people who would kidnap his retainers, cruelly torture them, and then feed them to monsters right in front of Rodrigo.

I had to instill in Stefan the idea that whenever he harmed Rodrigo, his daughter, Estella, would have to pay the price. It might have been unfair, like Stefan pointed out, but without such drastic measures, I would not even be able to see Rodrigo.

"But why do you want to meet him so badly?"

Back in my room, I told Jane about how I was going on a date. She tilted her head in confusion.

"Hm?" I stared at her, considering the unexpected question.

"You've officially announced that you two are dating, and you will get approval one day anyway. Is all this really necessary?"

Jane must have been accosted by the other servants, asking her to try and talk me out of it. It must have looked like I was adding fuel to the fire, when we could just wait it out now that we had announced our relationship and people had seen us getting along at the banquet.

"Love is nice and all, but it appears that you like him more than he likes you, and I don't think that's proper."

I smiled, assuring her I was all right, before quickly jumping into bed. I heard Jane clicking her tongue but pretended not to notice.

The empire was old-fashioned. Women could not go after a man or confess their affections first. All kinds of things were frowned upon when it came to women's behavior. This was limited to nobles, but still.

"Don't tell me Sir Rodrigo has something on you."

"Huh? On me?" I waved away her theory.

Jane narrowed her eyes and continued. "It's suspicious."

"What in the world do you mean?"

"It's strange that you fell in love with him at first sight," she prodded. "You never had any interest in men."

"He's handsome, though," I told her.

"That is true."

"And he's rich."

Jane did not disagree. *She has no choice but to agree.*

I kept going, smiling at her now, "And he's talented. Besides being an Erhart, he's perfect, don't you think?"

Jane pointed out that the main problem lay there. *This girl never lets anything go unchallenged.* I didn't respond this time, and so she went about her chores, tidying the room.

"Oh, right!" she said. "The crown prince has sent you a gift."

When I continued to lie there on my stomach, unmoving, Jane brought the gift over to me. Detheus had begun sending gifts to the manor since the day we'd met. His first gift was a hundred roses. They were beautiful, but since I didn't like the person who had sent them, I threw them in the trash without even smelling them.

And the next day, he sent jewels. The necklace gleamed with a sapphire pendant as big as my fist. But I had it sent back to the imperial palace immediately. *I'm already dating someone, so stop trying to win me over. That man has no principles whatsoever.*

"If it's expensive, send it back, and if not, just throw it away."

"You're not even going to look?"

"Why should I? It's better to put a stop to this early on," I said firmly.

Jane hummed and began ripping the box open. The relatively large box contained a lavish dress. The jewels embroidered on the dress glinted in the light.

"Wow," Jane said. "Will you really not look at it before you send it back?"

"Just send it back."

I got up from the bed and moved to my closet. I opened the closet door, slipping a piece of paper between two bricks on the wall inside. With a grinding sound, the bricks moved aside. The Kartina manor had many secret mechanisms like this.

I knew of quite a few secret mechanisms that even Stefan didn't know about. It helped that I had read the author's blog posts about these kinds of details. I took a box of poison bottles out of its hiding spot. Too busy searching for a potion to make more Shadow Gang pouches for Rodrigo, I missed my chance to tell Jane to stop when she said she would read the card.

"I thought of you while I stayed up all night designing this dress. Just imagining you in it takes my breath away. I would like you to wear this dress to the upcoming imperial banquet... *Eww.*" Jane shuddered.

Still, I was too busy making plans to build up Rodrigo's resistance to the Shadow Gang scent to pay her any mind.

"I shouldn't use too much right off the bat, should I?" I murmured, raising a vial as small as my pinky finger and shaking it. The main ingredient of the potion was a special plant that only grew on the Kartina property, so it was hard to make a large amount. Since my family didn't know I could make this type of potion, I had to find the ingredients in secret, and that was no small feat.

"My lady, what are you doing in the closet?" Jane asked.

"I'm looking for clothes!"

I was keeping it secret from Jane as well. The meeting between me and Rodrigo had to be nothing more than a date in her eyes—not a training session.

"You look beautiful today, as always, Estella."

He said, "as always," as if he had complimented me before. I placed my left hand on the one he offered me. As soon as I took it, I could feel intense gazes on my back.

"Do we have company?" Rodrigo asked.

"We're being tailed. Just pretend not to notice."

The day after the news of my date with Rodrigo had made it around the manor, Ada and Ayla hurried home without even completing their mission at the western border.

The only reason they had been able to make it back in a day when it took a week on horseback was because of the Kartina mages. With little money—and a lot of blackmail—the Kartinas employed several mages, rare in the empire.

Thanks to Ayla and Ada simply riling up the monsters and leaving, a village in the western region had been destroyed. In the end, Stefan had been called to the imperial palace and had to go to the west himself to take care of the situation. When he returned, there would be hell to pay at the Kartina manor.

"Thanks to that, there are only three people tailing us."

"Your mother must be busy."

"What, are you interested in my mom?" I teased.

Hela was attractive, and I wasn't just saying that because I was her daughter. She had pale white skin and a slim body, and her elegant movements and delicate voice made her seem much younger than she actually was. If Hela wanted, she could probably seduce a young man in his early twenties with no problem.

"I don't like disrespecting my elders. I simply asked because it seems easier to convince your mother than your father." Rodrigo stroked his chin. His face practically shone. His attitude made it clear that he was aware that his face was one of his greatest weapons.

"Use your looks somewhere else. Do you think good looks would work on someone who is really attractive themselves?" I whispered as we approached the carriage.

"Is that so? Is that why it does not work on you?" Rodrigo mumbled something confusing.

"What?"

Instead of answering, Rodrigo simply grinned at my response. "After you."

Rattle.

The carriage ride was anything but smooth, as expected. It looked as though Rodrigo had made sure the carriage was comfortable. Thanks to the numerous fluffy cushions, at least my tailbone didn't ache. Though he had sat down next to me as we left, Rodrigo moved to sit across from me once we had gotten farther away from the Kartina manor.

"Did anything else happen that day? Sir Stefan seemed quite angry."

You're the one who made him angry. If you're worried about me, please stop fighting with my dad. "Of course not. It was fine, he just pestered me all day."

"My apologies. I tried being courteous, but I kept slipping up."

"Why?" I was simply curious.

"I am not sure." Rodrigo placed his elbow on the windowsill and put his chin on his hand. He stared into my eyes as if he might find an answer there.

"Maybe," he started, "because you, the Kartinas' treasure, are on my side? I keep thinking I want to flaunt that in front of the other Kartinas."

Huh...?

"It made me realize I am pretty unhinged. Does that bother you?" Head bowed slightly, his eyes raised to meet mine, serious.

CHAPTER
TWENTY

That was the end of Rodrigo's confession. The atmosphere inside the carriage shifted uncomfortably. The carriage was well ventilated, but the air was heavy and thick.

I swallowed hard and responded in an overly chipper way, "It's all right. It's not as though we need to be courteous to each other."

I waved my hand dismissively and opened a window. I was worried that he would want to continue this conversation, but Rodrigo kept his mouth shut. Breathing in the fresh air, I fixed my gaze on the scenery outside. It was sunny, and a pleasant breeze wafted by. Behind our carriage, another tailed closely. It was ridiculous and gaudy, mimicking the style of the nouveau riche.

I was sure that Kalen, Ada, and Ayla were in it. They were usually so good at tailing people during missions, but today they were practically advertising their presence. It was the only weak point of the Kartinas, who were otherwise skilled at everything. When it came to me, they were so overly enthusiastic that their actions often resulted in outcomes far from what they had planned.

I wonder if this will lead to some embarrassment in the future.

"Have you thought about where you want our first date to take place?"

"Pardon?" I hadn't thought about it at all since I considered today to be a training session under the guise of a date.

"If you have not, how about we stick with my plans?"

"Sure, I don't mind." It didn't matter, as long as I could be alone with Rodrigo. I was more curious about what Kalen, Ada, and Ayla had planned than where we were going. Rodrigo kept talking, but I remained preoccupied.

The carriage kept moving. The horseman kept spurring on the horses, and the rattling of the carriage continued. We were getting farther and farther away from the city. *Didn't a date usually involve going to a famous cafe for tea and dessert, watching a play or an opera, or visiting an exhibit?*

I only turned to Rodrigo once the scenery outside turned completely green. For some reason, I had a bad feeling. I had to ask.

"Where are we going?"

"This is it."

The carriage had stopped by a hill where the breeze blew, tossing my hair. A river flowed at the foot of the hill. The sunshine bounced off the water and sparkled like gems. It was a magnificent view.

At the bottom of the hill was an enormous mansion— one no ordinary noble could even dream of—constructed in a foreign architectural style usually seen by the ocean. I could practically feel the ocean breeze just by standing there. I especially liked how well the white bricks and blue roof went together.

"What a pretty place."

"I agree. It's mine."

"Aha. You own a beautiful building in a nice place."

"Do you like it?"

There was no reason not to. It would be paradise to have a cup of tea on that balcony, feeling the breeze after sleeping in till noon.

I nodded. Rodrigo's lips spread into a pleasant smile.

"I am glad. Then let us move on."

What? We're not going in there? He's just showing off?

I wanted to enjoy the breeze some more, but Rodrigo ushered me back into the carriage.

Our next destination was a wide strip of land with dozens of greenhouses. Rodrigo led me to the biggest one. Inside, warmth wrapped over us, and a stifling humidity to accommodate the edible flowers that sprouted and bloomed around us. With a snap of Rodrigo's fingers, the windows along the roof opened simultaneously and made it a bit easier to breathe.

"Amazing technology."

"It's magic." Rodrigo corrected my comment and led me further in.

Flowers of every shade of the rainbow covered every surface. Before I knew it, I was looking around with my mouth open in amazement. I felt like a country bumpkin who had just moved to the big city. But it didn't matter. The wondrous, beautiful flowers just made me happy.

Gorgeous hues. Red, yellow, blue... it was like seeing an artist's colorful palette.

"Are they all edible?"

"Of course. Would you like to try one?"

As a response to my question, Rodrigo plucked a red petal and placed it between my lips. Then he also took a bite of the red flower. As I chewed on the petal, I noticed a slightly bitter taste. It definitely wasn't a good flavor. But the floral scent filling my mouth was nice. The downside was that it stained your mouth and tongue red.

"Would you like another?"

When Rodrigo offered, I didn't refuse. I was getting a bit hungry anyway. Expecting a typical date at a cafe, I only had a simple lunch, and it was now a suitable time for tea and refreshments. We walked around the greenhouse, each holding a big flower to chew on.

"Why are you growing flowers, though? And edible ones at that."

"I don't just grow edible ones. And I grow other things as well," Rodrigo began to explain. In the winter, vegetables were hard to come by. But nobles wanted vegetables even in the winter because they believed it to be proper to have an assortment of vegetables on the table, even though they mainly ate meat. As a result, the price of vegetables skyrockets every winter.

"We have made quite a profit. Even now, our earnings are remarkably high."

I see. I nodded my head, rather indifferent.

"Do you find it uninteresting?"

Rodrigo, who had been walking beside me, came to a halt. It took me a moment to notice, so I stopped a few steps ahead of him.

"Why?"

He stepped closer. The casual air around him had dissipated. His eyes were as deep as the abyss as he looked down at me. My heart fluttered. I wanted to avoid his gaze, but we were on a narrow walkway with nowhere to hide. My eyes wandered before focusing on a particular spot. A smile crept onto my lips.

"There's something on your face," I said, pointing at Rodrigo.

The edible flower from before had left a red stain above the left corner of his lips. Rodrigo raised his hand to his mouth.

"Where? Here?"

"No, not there."

"Here?"

I began to grow frustrated as he kept missing the spot. "Stay still for a moment."

I closed the distance between us. Getting on my tiptoes, I placed my hand on the spot above his mouth. His lips were warm. So warm that I was worried about his health.

Rodrigo, who I thought would remove my hand immediately, fixed his gaze on me and simply watched what I was doing. I could have just shown him where it was, but I began to try and wipe away the stain in the same way I had wiped away the monster blood on Stefan. But it was harder than I thought.

Will it come off if I rub harder? I immediately dropped that thought. Rodrigo's lips had turned bright red, even though I didn't rub them very hard. It seemed like I would draw blood if I rubbed harder.

Should I use my spit? My spit on his lips...? I pictured a young couple pressing their lips together.

"What are you thinking about?"

I thought this every time I heard it, but his voice was very nice. It was a low pitch that echoed deep in my soul. The sensation of his lips moving under my fingers was unfamiliar and strange.

"Not... much."

"Is that so?" he said with a small sigh.

"It's not coming off. Will you lean closer?"

It was hard to stay on my tiptoes. Now that he knew where the spot was, I could have left it to him, but I was determined.

As Rodrigo leaned down, his face fell into shadow. It was difficult to see the red stain that had gotten lighter, so I leaned in closer as well. My eyelashes trembled as Rodrigo's breath brushed over them.

I could feel each breath he took. The world hushed around us, and I could almost hear the blood pumping through my veins. And my heart was thumping wildly... or was it his? And just as his gaze was starting to overwhelm me—

Boom!

There was a sudden explosion of sound.

Crash!

The noise continued. The panels of glass on the greenhouse ceiling shattered, one by one, raining slicing shards down on us. Rodrigo immediately took off his jacket and placed it over my head.

"It's my brother."

Kalen had thrown a bomb. My heart dropped into my stomach.

The pretty greenhouse had been wrecked in the blink of an eye. The delicious flowers withered, some burning in the heat of the explosion. Even if some were unharmed, the shards of glass everywhere would make it impossible to sell them now.

"I'm sorry, Rodrigo. I'll pay for everything."

"There's no need."

Rodrigo's words were firm. At his almost cold tone, I studied his face. This time—well, every time, really—Kalen, Ada, and Ayla were in the wrong. I thought they might shoot some arrows, but I didn't expect them to blow up a whole greenhouse.

"What a pity." Rodrigo drew his hand away from my shoulder. I was concerned about his hair, which was left disheveled after running with me in his arms. Noticing my stare, he asked, "Do I look bad now?"

Not at all.

Even with bedhead, Rodrigo would still look handsome. He ran a hand through his tousled hair.

"I'm so sorry," I told him. "It's such an expensive greenhouse too, I'm sure."

I didn't know much about business, but I was at least aware of the fact that the amount of technology required to operate a greenhouse like this was exorbitantly expensive. Anyone would be able to tell.

"I am not upset because the greenhouse was destroyed. I am upset that my gift was ruined."

A gift?

Oh, I see. He must have wanted to gift these flowers to someone.

"I don't know who it is for, but I apologize."

Rodrigo let out a chuckle.

Why is he laughing? He's able to laugh after his greenhouse was just blown up? How nice of him.

It was hard to believe that a man like this would go berserk.

"Estella, I just had a thought."

"Yes, Rodrigo, what is it?"

"I believe we really need to talk."

Of course, we do. We need to discuss compensation after all. There are so many things to reimburse him for.

"But before that, it looks like we must calm down your brother first."

As Rodrigo stepped forward, an iron mace came flying toward his face.

"Take that as well."

"This? A bomb? Are you planning to blow up a whole street in the middle of town?"

Ada nodded at Kalen's question. "Yes. Take it with you, dear brother."

Ada and Ayla usually spoke casually with Kalen, but they would call him "dear brother" when they were particularly irritated. She said it just now in a sarcastic tone, in an attempt to irritate Kalen just as much as she was. Kalen placed the bomb Ada threw at him into a bag.

"Are you going out to hunt monsters?" The butler, who was bringing the siblings tea, paused. It was strange that Ayla and Ada, who had just returned from hunting monsters, were heading out again so soon.

"No, not hunting." Ayla smiled darkly as she polished Ada's sword.

"Then what is the purpose of all these weapons...?" The butler took a closer look at all the items littering the floor. A set of ten A-level poisons that had to be handled with care, an iron mace that looked too heavy to carry, smoke bombs and others bombs powerful enough to blow up an entire mansion... they were definitely preparing to hunt monsters. But the words that came out of Ayla's mouth were entirely unexpected.

"We're following Estella on her date."

At that point in time, Kalen had no intention of using the bombs. If Rodrigo did something bad to Estella, he planned on simply slitting his throat. This was because Estella didn't like loud noises. *I really don't want to use the bombs!*

"He planned that, didn't he? That bastard."

The location of the date was strange. It looked like he was kidnapping her, the way they kept getting further away from town. When they finally arrived at the isolated mansion, Kalen immediately pictured Rodrigo locking her away and doing horrible things to her.

Whips, ropes... why is that all I can think of?!

Just as Ada was cursing up a storm and ready to pounce, Rodrigo and Estella got back into the carriage.

"I guess this isn't the place."

It made sense since a kidnapper would stop by different locations to throw off pursuers before heading to the final destination.

"Let's wait. We have to find his base of operations."

If we destroy that, I'm sure it will make things difficult for Rodrigo. We might as well crush his head with an iron mace while we're at it.

The second location was a greenhouse. The two of them went inside together. Unable to follow them, Kalen, Ada, and Ayla climbed onto the roof.

The three of them lay down on the glass and moved carefully. Just one wrong move would send them tumbling to the ground. There were a few close moments, but they kept watching.

Out of all the food in the world, why is he feeding her damn flowers? Kalen repressed the anger that bubbled up. They had decided to wait a bit longer when the atmosphere around those two turned suggestive. Estella approached him first. That by itself was already hard to accept, but then Estella raised her hand to touch Rodrigo's face. And then Rodrigo leaned toward her!

"Did you light it?" Kalen held out his hand to Ayla behind him.

"It's ready." Ayla attached the bomb to the greenhouse roof with a frosty expression.

All three of them leaned back and backflipped off the roof. As soon as they landed on the ground, the greenhouse collapsed with a loud boom.

CHAPTER
TWENTY-ONE

"Estella... Estella!"

Kalen, Ayla, and Ada ran into the ruined greenhouse, and at the same time, the Erhart knights emerged from their hiding spots.

"Assassins! Protect His Grace!"

Kalen leapt into action, throwing shuriken at the knights who were rushing in. He must have thought it would be hard to reach me once the knights surrounded me, because he hurriedly jumped into the fray. He was throwing shuriken left and right while swinging his iron mace.

Crack!

I heard something break after making contact with his iron mace. I saw Kalen initially giggling, but his expression quickly shifted to a scowl. He was furious. It was obvious who that fury was aimed at.

Rodrigo.

I suddenly felt sorry for him. Stepping onto the knights' shoulders, Kalen leapt into the air. Then he caught sight of me, wrapped in Rodrigo's jacket.

Please stop, Kalen. I mouthed my plea, but Kalen failed to get the message.

"Arghhh!" Kalen let out a war cry and threw a shuriken at Rodrigo. Fluttering petals and sprays of blood. A surreal scene unfolded around me. The Kartinas could no longer be stopped.

Estella had to watch from the sidelines as Ayla, Ada, and Kalen fought Rodrigo.

The three siblings were struggling, far outnumbered by the Erhart knights—and Rodrigo's fighting abilities exceeded expectations. The Kartinas, who had counted on having the upper hand or at least an equal footing, were slowly being pushed back.

Just as Kalen was about to turn around and slit the throat of a knight coming at him from behind, a dagger came flying out of nowhere at a tremendous speed and knocked his sword away. The dagger managed to change the trajectory of Kalen's sword and save the knight's life.

What was that?

An attack with such precision amidst the chaos of the fight was no mean feat.

They've got an ace up their sleeve. When did the Erhart knights get so skilled?

As Kalen contemplated this, his gaze fell on Estella, who was pale as a sheet. Above her head, a steel beam was about to fall.

"Estella!" Kalen cried out. He kicked away a knight that tried to close in on him and swung his iron mace at everyone blocking his way.

"Estella, watch out!"

Perhaps she heard him. Estella's eyes met his, but she didn't move. Kalen was frustrated. The steel beam above Estella's head creaked and wavered, as if it was about to crash on top of her.

"Ada! Ayla!" Kalen shouted.

The twins quickly realized what was happening and leapt toward Estella. But there was someone who was sprinting toward Estella even faster. Yet again, it was Rodrigo.

"Everyone, evacuate!" Rodrigo had instinctively realized that the remainder of the greenhouse would not hold up much longer after the impact of the explosion.

"But Your Grace, the assassins—"

"Everyone, evacuate! I can take care of myself!" Rodrigo snapped back.

Estella was in danger. It irritated him that he had to take care of his men first.

Why isn't she running away? What is she planning? Rodrigo shook his head, ridding himself of his questions. He had to focus on saving her. *I hope she doesn't get hurt.*

Creak.

The steel beams above emitted ugly sounds as they began to collapse in on each other. The noise grew louder. Any second, the beams would fully collapse. The remaining glass shards rained onto the ground. Then, a steel beam began to fall right on top of Estella.

"Estella!"

All four of them cried out her name in unison.

Crash!

The greenhouse collapsed. The whole structure morphed into an unrecognizable pile of rubble.

"Your Grace..."

The Erhart knights were in tears. They could still hear Rodrigo's last words, telling them to evacuate, echoing in their heads.

"His Grace saved u-us, and..."

Sniff!

Grief was infectious. The knights, as burly as they were, set aside their shame and let their tears flow freely at the thought of having lost their benevolent master.

"O-over there!" Their sobs became wails when suddenly, a young knight jumped up and down, pointing at a pile of rubble.

"What is it? Do you see something? What?"

The knights quickly pulled themselves together, wiped their tears, and turned to the pile of rubble. They could see movement.

"Your Grace... no... the Kartinas!"

The three Kartinas got to their feet. They were carrying Rodrigo. Kalen was holding up his legs while Ada and Ayla each supported his shoulders.

I realized that the greenhouse was about to collapse during the middle of the fight. Just as my siblings began their rampage. I wanted everyone to get out safely, but the fighting had to stop for that to happen. And there was only one way to do that—get everyone's attention on me.

Without a moment's hesitation, I reached under my dress to unsheathe the dagger strapped to my thigh. I threw it toward Kalen. Just as expected, he caught sight of me and ran in my direction. Ada, Ayla, and Rodrigo followed suit.

Rodrigo was quick to notice. He ordered his knights to get out. All I had to do was leave at the right moment. Everything was going smoothly, but there was just one thing that defied my expectations. The greenhouse collapsed faster than I had anticipated.

The last thing I saw was my siblings shielding me and Rodrigo's shocked expression.

Rumble... Crash!

I was safe, thanks to my siblings shielding me. My body had been jostled, and I felt something hit me, but it didn't hurt.

But what about them? Even the Kartinas, with their abnormal strength, would be greatly injured by a heavy steel beam hitting them from such a height.

"Ugh." But all they did was let out a small groan.

How?

It was only once the greenhouse had completely collapsed that I could see the reason. Once the dust had settled and the glass shards that had been raining down all hit the ground. And after my siblings let go of me.

"Rodrigo!"

Rodrigo lay on the ground on his side.

"Rodrigo! Rodrigo? Can you hear me? What happened?"

He had gone deathly pale. His easygoing smile was still there, but he seemed completely exhausted.

"He put up a shield."

Rodrigo wasn't in any condition to speak, and so Ayla answered for him. She sounded furious, but the usual murderous edge of her tone was absent.

"Damn it! We could have saved Estella even without your dumb shield." Kalen snapped at Rodrigo, still flat on the ground. I should have been feeling thankful, but I was consumed with resentment toward myself for causing this situation.

"Everyone!" As I sat next to Rodrigo, who struggled to breathe, I turned to look up at my siblings. Ayla, Ada, and Kalen all drew in a sharp breath. I was angry at them. But I couldn't help but think it was all my fault. Had I really not known that my siblings would act this way? Had I not even suspected that their deep love for me, their twisted nature, would lead to catastrophe? Instead of snapping at them, I sighed. "Please carry Rodrigo to the carriage. Quickly."

I had to get him home. He seemed unharmed on the outside, but there was a good chance he had internal injuries. Rodrigo was not a practiced mage. Until he went berserk at the end of the novel, his magic always came with serious side effects.

He had collapsed no doubt because he had used magic, straining his body to protect us.

"All right..."

Ada, Ayla, and Kalen, who seemed to have finally realized the gravity of the situation, responded quietly.

"I'm tired."

Rodrigo was lying down inside the carriage with his head on my lap. The carriage may have been large, but there was nowhere near enough room for him to stretch out properly. He had to lie on his side uncomfortably with his knees drawn up.

"Sleep." I had to hold onto him tightly so he wouldn't fall forward whenever the carriage bounced on the uneven road. Otherwise, he would topple onto the floor.

"I don't sleep in front of people... no, I never even get sleepy. How strange."

I looked down at Rodrigo. He had turned over to lie on his back. His long legs were drawn up.

"Is it the Shadow Gang's scent pouch?" he asked.

The way his voice cracked made my heart ache. I told him, "I haven't even started your scent immunity training yet.

You must be tired because you used too much magic, so just go to sleep."

"Strange... how strange," he mumbled, blinking slowly.

What's so strange? He should just sleep if he's tired. Does he want me to sing him a lullaby or something? Or does he need a stuffed animal? What a difficult man. I buried my worries for him in my pointed complaints.

"I've never once slept in peace," Rodrigo suddenly confessed.

"Pardon?"

"Someone could attack me anywhere, at any moment."

I quietly closed my mouth again. It was heart wrenching. Rodrigo had been exposed to deadly threats from an incredibly young age. The empire's only archduke family was a prime target. Knowing the barbaric nature of this world, it was clear what this entailed, and it made me feel sorry for him.

"There's a carriage full of Kartinas behind us, so is it safe for me to sleep on the lap of a Kartina...?"

The question seemed rhetorical because Rodrigo closed his eyes as if he already knew the answer.

"It's all right, go to sleep. I told you I would protect you." I ran my hand through his disheveled hair as I reassured him.

CHAPTER
TWENTY-TWO

Rodrigo tried his best to stay awake, but his eyes felt heavy. He was being followed by the Kartinas, and that was enough to make him tense. Even on a regular day, whenever the Kartinas' movements seemed suspicious, he would stay up all night, his sword within reach.

When he did try to rest, Rodrigo was never able to fall into a deep sleep. He would wake up every few hours throughout the night, check outside his windows, and strain his ears for any sounds. Only after such precautions was he able to take short naps.

He thought he had gotten used to it. He would have to live like this his whole life, so he had given up on restful sleep. He had even been afraid to sleep at times. But today, he just wanted to let everything go, to let sleep wash over him.

What if I die here? With my head on the lap of this interesting woman with a sweet scent... maybe this isn't a bad way to go.

It must be because he felt so weak. Rodrigo chided himself for thinking such nonsense, closing his eyes, before his consciousness faded completely. It had been a long time since he had fallen into such a deep sleep.

"Estella! Let's go home—"

Shh!

Rodrigo's carriage came to a halt in front of the gates of the Erhart manor. Kalen hurriedly opened the carriage door. He surveyed the scene, shocked beyond words. I could tell what had rendered him speechless just by his expression.

It must be the sight of Rodrigo sleeping on my lap.

Kalen looked like he was about to cry out, so I raised my hand to shush him. "Go home, Kalen. Take Ada and Ayla with you. I'll head home once Rodrigo wakes up."

"How hurt could he—*mmph*."

I shot him a vicious glare.

"Th-then I'll stay with you too!" Kalen quickly offered, but I shook my head. The whole way here, I had been thinking about what Rodrigo had said just before he fell asleep.

"There's a carriage full of Kartinas behind us, so is it safe for me to sleep on the lap of a Kartina...?"

His voice had trailed off as he had said this, but his words were etched into my memory like a tattoo. One of his hands was still resting near his sword.

He was never able to rest easy. And all because of the Kartinas, who had continuously tormented his family. It was better to keep the Kartinas as far away as possible while he was recovering.

But what about me? My heart lurched.

"Go home. We'll talk about what happened today when I get back."

Kalen slumped his shoulders. He moved his lips silently, his expression making it evident that he had a lot to say.

"If anything happens, blow your whistle."

In other words, he wasn't going to enter the manor, but he would be waiting nearby. The Kartinas all owned a special whistle used to signal their locations in case of emergencies.

The sound this whistle made was at a pitch only a trained hawk could hear, allowing the Kartinas to locate each other without anyone else knowing.

"All right."

I wanted them all to return home, but I decided to settle for them not entering the Erhart manor. The reason my siblings weren't acting up right now wasn't because they approved of my relationship with Rodrigo, but because he had been injured while saving us. Kalen closed the carriage door, still looking like he had something left to say. The carriage continued onto the Erhart manor grounds—with just me and Rodrigo.

"What happened?"

Rodrigo's right-hand men, Gunther, Devlon, and Augus, came running toward the carriage. They looked worried, apparently already aware of what had happened at the greenhouse. Gunther immediately began interrogating me as soon as I stepped out of the carriage.

If any of the other Kartinas had witnessed this, he would have been impaled right there and then, but fortunately, my siblings were far enough away.

"There was an accident. Sir Rodrigo used too much magic."

"Magic?" Augus asked in disbelief.

"Yes, would it be all right to tell you the specifics later? We have to get Rodrigo to his bed quickly."

"Did he collapse? I mean, did he faint?" Devlon piped up.

"Oh! No. He was talking to me inside the carriage and fell asleep after saying he was sleepy."

Gunther, Devlon, and Augus stared at me, eyes wide.

Are they worried because Rodrigo was hurt? But no, it looked more like they were confused.

"H-has he died?" Gunther opened the carriage door.

"I'm alive." Rodrigo, who must have woken up in the meantime, was sitting upright. Gunther quickly backed away and pushed Devlon forward. *I knew Rodrigo must not be feeling well.* Judging by the way Gunther and Devlon were acting, it seemed to be true.

Rodrigo stepped off the carriage, stretching lazily. There was no sign of fatigue or irritation on his face whatsoever.

"Is it all right for you to just walk around like this? Don't you have your family doctor? We should call him." I was worried about Rodrigo. But despite all my worries, he seemed completely fine after his nap. *Still*, I thought, *you never know.* I stepped closer to him to try and support his weight. I could feel him chuckling above my head.

"I'm twice as big as you." Rodrigo whispered, "If I lean on you, you will collapse."

"Then don't put your full weight on me." I was well aware that I wouldn't be able to carry even a single leg of his. I wasn't strong, but I was skilled. I could knock him over, but I wouldn't be able to carry him. But I still wanted to help him, even if it was just a little.

"I'm all right, Estella. For once, I was able to sleep well." His voice was very clear. It seemed just a bit of good sleep had been enough for Rodrigo to recover completely.

A handsome blond man was seated in the emperor's secret meeting room. He was lithe and pale, as though he had never seen the sun, and his unusually red, beautiful lips made it difficult to assume his gender at first glance. When he got to his feet, his thin but tall frame with wide-set shoulders was revealed, delicate veins tracing his large hands.

"Y-Your Holiness, please sit down."

Emperor Thereo quickly got up and followed Pope Nathaniel. Nathaniel leisurely walked toward the windows, peering outside. The northern tower of the imperial palace was incredibly tall and revealed a different view with every step you climbed.

"Did you feel that just now?"

"Pardon? Feel what?"

Nathaniel clicked his tongue. The emperor, the descendant of the man who had been loved by a goddess, was weak. He was extremely irritated that it was his job to protect this man. But he was a servant of the gods, and the gods had rescued him from the dirty slums. So, as long as he didn't have to put himself in danger, Nathaniel had to aid the emperor.

"Erhart's magic," he said. "It seems as though there is an issue with the seal."

"Oh..." Thereo was unable to find the words to reply, so he just stood there, slack-jawed. Nathaniel was kind enough to tell him what had to be done.

"What could have caused this issue?" As long as he wasn't a complete idiot, anyone would be able to infer what he was saying.

"I shall find out!" Thereo hurried out of the room.

Thank goodness. At least the man I must serve is not a complete idiot. Nathaniel smiled wryly as he stared into the void. The tea on the table was still warm.

At my urging, Rodrigo was forced to call the Erharts' doctor, Heffolk.

"You are in perfect condition. Did you really get injured?" Heffolk made his diagnosis after poking and prodding Rodrigo, who was obediently lying on his bed.

"Are you really, really sure he's fine?" I asked before Rodrigo could respond. "A big steel beam crashed onto Rodrigo. Onto his magic shield, to be precise."

"Yes."

"No internal injuries either?"

Heffolk's eyes narrowed as he looked at me. I could practically hear what he was thinking. *Who are you? Why are you so interested in our master's wellbeing?*

Come to think of it, everyone at the Erhart manor seemed to be full of suspicion. Gunther certainly was, just like Heffolk, and Augus wasn't very sympathetic, either.

It must be because I'm a Kartina.

Heffolk was staring at me, waiting for my answer.

"I am Sir Rodrigo's..." I trailed off, unsure of how to introduce myself.

"She's my lover." Rodrigo suddenly spoke up. He grasped my wrist and pulled me closer to the bed. I flopped down next to him. Rodrigo looked up at Heffolk as he caressed my wrist with his thumb.

"My lover asked you a question. Are you not going to answer?"

Whenever he referred to me as "my lover" in that pleasant voice, a strange feeling rushed over me. A shiver of goosebumps and a flutter in my chest.

Anyway, it was different from usual. I wasn't the only one who noticed something was off. The faces of everyone gathered in the bedroom were indescribable. *Have none of you ever dated? You guys are overreacting. Not that I'm not overreacting.* I let out a small chuckle at the thought.

Rodrigo's thumb paused. He looked over at me. Our gazes intertwined.

"Isn't it getting hot in here?"

I could hear Gunther talking to Devlon.

"I really want to leave," Devlon whispered.

"No internal injuries either. But just in case, it would be better for you to rest, Your Grace. May we take our leave?" Heffolk asked after clearing his throat.

"Go ahead." Rodrigo waved his hand dismissively, his eyes still fixed on me. I could hear everyone rushing out.

I should get going too. I tried to get off the bed, but Rodrigo held onto my wrist, tightening his grasp. I asked, "What is it? Didn't you say we could leave?"

"Not you. It would look strange if my lover left right away, would it not? A lover would usually stay and take care of the patient in this situation."

Usually? Ha, he must have a lot of experience. With a petulant expression, I shook his hand off and crossed my arms.

"Did your other lovers do that?"

"Other lovers?"

"Yes."

Rodrigo kept his mouth shut, seemingly confused about what I was asking. Then he let out a laugh. "You're the first," he said solemnly.

Since he was lying down, his hair lay flat away from his face, allowing me to see his handsome face more clearly.

"First what?" I replied curtly.

"My first lover, my first dating experience, the first person I've fallen asleep next to, and…" It seemed like he had something important to add after that "and." He closed his mouth as if he was unable to continue.

"And?" I impatiently urged him to complete his sentence. He stared at me for a short while, hesitating before he spoke.

"And the first person I want to make up excuses for to keep by my side."

I trembled. It felt like I had heard some great declaration, but it wasn't entirely welcome. His words were like a great wave, and that wave was moving quickly toward me.

TWENTY-THREE

"I'm sorry, Estella. It's my fault. I will never do anything like this again." Kalen, on his knees, was begging for forgiveness.

"That's weird." Ayla shook her head and gestured for him to try again.

"Estella, from now on, I'll only torment that bastard a little bit. I won't hurt him."

"Are you trying to provoke her?"

Kalen, Ada, and Ayla were hiding in the shadows of the outer walls of the Erhart manor and thinking of ways to appease Estella's anger. They had already gone over ten different versions, but none of them had been unanimously approved. *Will we ever be able to appease Estella at this rate?* Their chances of success seemed faint.

"Come on! What else are we supposed to say? Why did that bastard have to go and save us?"

"Save us? Please. He just butted in unnecessarily."

As Kalen and Ayla spoke, Ada stuck her hand out in between them, interjecting, "Let's be honest... he did help us."

Kalen and Ayla swiveled their heads around to look at Ada. Their eyes blazed. "So what? Are you saying you approve of Rodrigo now?"

They're so simple-minded. How do you even get such a black and white mindset? Ayla sighed before she spoke. "Haven't you ever heard of 'one step back, two steps forward?'"

Kalen piped up, "Let's change our strategies. From now on, no insulting Rodrigo in front of Estella. And let's try not to interfere when they're together."

Ayla grimaced, as if she hated every suggestion.

"Instead, let's think of another way to screw him over. We've got to use our brains."

"Ha..." Kalen let out a sigh. The way they were behaving was very uncharacteristic of the Kartinas. But because this involved Estella, they were unable to see things straight. And their opponent wasn't a pushover either. Now they had to fight like Kartinas.

"That mine of his that blew up... it hasn't been restored yet, right?" Ada chuckled ominously.

Kalen knew exactly what she meant. "I'll get the kindling."

If there was trouble in his territory, he would have to investigate it himself. Out of sight, out of mind, they say. And if the crown prince takes that time to make his move, then even better.

For the first time in a long time, Kalen, Ada, and Ayla had felt optimistic.

"Welcome home, Estella!" My siblings greeted me. It was well past sunset when I got back to the Kartina manor.

It wasn't because Rodrigo had held me back. He had said a lot of strange things before falling asleep again. I really didn't have the chance to look after him properly, like he said I should. I simply watched him sleep, not realizing how much time had passed.

Before I knew it, it had gotten pretty late. It was hard to leave his side, but I had to return home.

"We're sorry, Estella."

Until I walked up to my room, Kalen, Ada, and Ayla followed me and recited a series of apologies. They seemed ready to get on their knees if I asked. I was unable to stay angry at them because they seemed genuinely sorry for what they had done. They had promised me something important, after all.

"We won't do it again."

It was an unexpectedly good outcome. But the one who deserved an apology was Rodrigo, not me. I knew that my siblings had done this out of love. And in the end, we were family.

But Rodrigo wasn't.

"You should apologize to Rodrigo," I told them, toning down a little bit.

"Of course! We've prepared a gift. We're going to give it to him at the upcoming banquet."

"The banquet?"

"That's right, Estella. The banquet at the imperial palace. The emperor ordered us to attend this time."

As far as I remember, Rodrigo doesn't like banquets. Will he be there?

"Because the pope will be there."

The pope? Who was he again? I tried to remember the story.

Maybe it was because it had been so long since I was reborn into this world, or because I had skimmed over a lot of the violent parts, but there were a few details in the novel I couldn't remember. *I think he was an important character...*

"Wouldn't it be good for Rodrigo to meet the pope?"

Kalen interrupted my train of thought. The papal court had a substantial role in the empire. Some legal proceedings, such as marriage or divorce, had to go through the papal court.

There was no reason for me to skip this banquet now that I had made my debut. I would have to convince Hela and Stefan, but that wouldn't be a problem.

I wanted to see the pope's face. If I did, there was a chance I would remember. *Should I attend as well? They said Rodrigo would be there too.*

"Let me escort you, Estella."

What about Rodrigo?

Ayla and Ada elbowed Kalen from each side.

"Uh, I mean, if you would let me." *Instead of Rodrigo,* Kalen added through gritted teeth.

I held off on an answer and shooed them out of my room. The word "pope" was stuck in my head. Anxiety quickened my pulse. I was overwhelmed by the ominous feeling that something terrible was going to happen at this banquet.

Stefan, who had left to take care of the monsters terrorizing the western border, was unable to return before the banquet.

"The monsters are behaving strangely."

Hela's expression turned solemn at the knight commander's report. The monsters that lived by the western border were not particularly aggressive or strong, hence why she often sent just her children to take care of them. *But they're still fighting back, even with Stefan there?*

"Get backup troops ready in case Stefan calls for them. How much mana can we extract from the mages?"

"Enough to conjure about five portals."

Mages were stuck-up and expensive to hire. Usually, in order to use essential magic such as transportation portals, the mages needed to be coaxed into helping. But the Kartinas used a different method.

Their method of choice was worthy of their title as a villain family. They had kidnapped and imprisoned some mages. A magic circle for the portals would be drawn up ahead of time, and all they had to do was extract the amount of mana needed from the mages. Extracting mana required a highly advanced technique, but the Kartinas owned a dark magic tome that had been handed down for generations. It detailed the precise way to extract mana.

"All right, go and kidnap a few more mages from the continent. We may need more gates," Hela commanded, unfeeling. She stood and threw the doors open wide. Her intense expression melted and stretched into a beaming smile.

"Welcome, Estella!" Hela said. "Let's go shopping!"

Gramlin, the Kartina knight commander, felt his skin crawl at her complete change in demeanor.

"Give me everything from here to there. Actually, no. I'll just buy the whole building."

The boutique's owner, Yves Saint Laura, whose designs were highly sought after in the empire, was clearly surprised at the box of gold bars Hela set down as she spoke.

"Th-the building isn't mine. But I will have everything wrapped up for you."

"There's no need."

Hela clapped her hands, and a number of Kartina servants appeared out of nowhere. They began to sweep everything on the shelves into boxes. Yves Saint Laura's jaw dropped open. From jewelry that commoners couldn't even dream of being able to afford, to dresses that even nobles had to queue up for, everything was packed into boxes.

"Mom, this is too much." I grabbed Hela's arm.

"Nonsense, Estella. It's not enough."

"Mom, I would have to get changed ten times a day if I wanted to wear all of these clothes."

"You just need to wear one dress. You can give the rest to whoever you want, at the end of the season, that is."

Yves Saint Laura's expression was priceless as she listened to our conversation. I shook my head. "Then why are you buying so much?"

"Why? Because no one in the empire can wear a dress by the same designer as you, of course. From now on, only you can wear Yves Saint Laura's dresses. As long as she is the best designer of the empire."

Hela glanced over at Yves Saint Laura. The boutique owner's face had gone completely serious. I bit my lower lip.

This is way too much.

I was sure that she had just spent most of the Kartinas' annual budget buying all of this, but there was no stopping Hela. And if I did stop her, she might not let me attend the banquet—so I wouldn't. I reminded myself that, in exchange for attending the ball, I had agreed to accept all of Hela's gifts.

I shouldn't have done that. But there was no use regretting it now.

"So which dress will you wear, Estella?" Hela asked.

On the day of the banquet, I picked out a dress that reminded me of cherry blossoms from among the many Yves Saint Laura dresses Hela had bought me. It was a dress without any adornments, made from fabric in different gradients of pink, with different shapes of fabric layered into a full skirt below the waist.

The delicate fabric fluttered around me like fairy wings with every movement. I was quite happy with the design, which drew attention to itself by its silhouette alone. The dress was somehow simple, but showy, modest but eye-catching, and looked expensive without being bejeweled.

"Wow, I've only ever heard about Yves Saint Laura, but this is amazing." The design was enough to impress even Jane, who had no interest in dresses. "I heard people sell their houses to buy one of these. Now I understand why."

Are her dresses really that expensive?

When I turned to look at Jane, she shrugged. "I don't know the exact price, either."

It did look expensive. But seeing that she had bought everything inside the store, I couldn't even imagine how much money Hela had spent.

"What kind of jewelry will you wear? It seems like a waste not to wear the sapphire necklace the crown prince sent you before."

"There are plenty of other necklaces over there." I gestured to a pile of open jewelry boxes lining the floor, waiting for me to make my choice.

"Hm, I guess so, but that sapphire was huge."

"Do you need a huge gemstone?" A voice that didn't belong here rang out from the window.

TWENTY-FOUR

Jane had picked up a knife and was about to throw it.

"Jane! It's Sir Rodrigo!" I cried out.

"Oh, is it?" Jane shrugged and turned away nonchalantly.

That was close. I sometimes suspected that Jane might have a drop of Kartina blood in her, judging by the way she tended to act first and explain later.

Rodrigo began climbing into the room. I hurried over to the window and looked around outside before dragging him all the way inside and slamming the window shut.

"What brings you all the way here?" I asked. *It's quiet outside, so he must have snuck in, but how?* He was dressed lightly, not a rope or grappling hook in sight.

"Magic." Rodrigo stuck out his fingers nonchalantly, and a blue light flickered into existence at their tips.

Was he always this skilled at magic? Teleporting with magic was difficult, even over short distances. I narrowed my eyes and looked at him.

"I cannot teleport to precise locations yet." That was why he had come through the window, he added, asking casually whether I agreed that it was pretty good for his first try, and then he handed me a box.

"It sounded like you were trying to decide on a necklace. I hope this will be a good answer."

A *present*? I opened the lid.

"Wow..." I let out an exclamation. "A rose made from a ruby?"

"You seemed to like roses," he replied.

"And it's very big."

"Do you like big gemstones? Next time, I'll get you one that's as big as a house."

"No, thank you. This looks quite expensive, gifts like this are too much."

"Oh. There's more, though." He bit his lower lip for a moment, as if troubled, before rummaging inside his jacket. "It isn't in great condition, but since I wanted you to have it, I am giving it to you anyway. If you do not like it, please do with it as you wish."

He held out an envelope full of documents. I handed the jewelry box to Jane. Judging by the way her face lit up, there was no doubt that she liked the necklace as well.

"What is this?"

"See for yourself."

I took the documents out of the envelope and skimmed through them. My eyes widened. *Did I read that wrong?*

My name was still there, even after I rubbed my eyes. The owner of the unique mansion Rodrigo had shown me, and the land surrounding it, as well as the greenhouses and the land around them, and even the ruby mine, was me!

Estella Kartina!

"I wanted to give this to you that day, but never got around to it. Do you like it?" Rodrigo asked when I didn't say anything.

What do you mean, do I like it? The scale of this gift was beyond imagination. The presents that Detheus had sent me were jaw-dropping, but this man was on another level.

I had assured him he could freely transfer ownership of his assets to me, but I didn't think he would do it so quickly. I stuttered, unable to find words, when Jane elbowed me and smiled brightly.

"My lady seems a bit shocked by this generous gift. I'm saying this from fifteen years of experience at her side. She definitely likes it." Jane quickly made sure I didn't have a chance to refuse.

Jane, you're quick. I'll give you that.

"I'll... take good care of it all and give it all back later." That was all I could say. Rodrigo furrowed his eyebrows, but we were unable to continue our conversation.

Knock, knock. Someone at the door.

"Estella, are you ready?" Ayla and Ada had come to pick me up so we could head out to the banquet.

"I'll look forward to seeing you." Rodrigo opened the window and disappeared.

Watching as he left, I stood there for a moment holding the documents in a daze, before coming to my senses and looking out the window. I caught a glimpse of the corner of his cape before it disappeared past the roof.

Kalen escorted me instead of Rodrigo. The night before, it had occurred to me that I had only been thinking of Rodrigo lately, and that the Kartinas must be feeling neglected. If I continued to focus only on Rodrigo, they might cause another catastrophe.

I also liked spending time with my siblings. Kalen, Ada, and Ayla beamed.

"The last banquet was ruined by Rodrigo, so let's enjoy ourselves this time, Estella," Kalen said.

Ada elbowed him hard in the side.

"It's all right," I told them. "As long as Rodrigo isn't around, you can speak freely."

They looked only a little sheepish.

"No cursing him out, though," I added, and smiled.

The awkward moment soon turned pleasant when I changed the subject.

"Oh right, you saw back then, right? The Erhart mansion and the greenhouses?"

"Hm? We saw the greenhouses, but what mansion?" Ayla feigned innocence. When I narrowed my eyes at her, Ada cleared her throat.

"You... knew?" Kalen asked. He omitted the words "that we were tailing you."

How could I not? With a ridiculous-looking carriage like that.

"They're mine now."

"*What?*" All three of them yelled at once. Seeing them practically jump out of their seats made me realize just how incredible Rodrigo's gifts were.

"I said they're all mine." *So don't mess with them.* The warning was implied.

"Y-you mean Rodrigo gave you all that?"

It was a gift, and an enormous one at that. I thought Kalen would be happy about it, but he shook with fury.

"Kalen?"

"What else?" he asked.

"A ruby mine."

"Arghhh!" Kalen grabbed his hair at the roots and shook his head. "Estella, you have to return it all. I'll work hard and get you something even better."

Ada and Ayla chimed in as well. "He's right, if we really put our minds to it, buying a mine is no problem."

I didn't ask how they were going to make that much money. There were many ways. Blackmail, murder, fraud... they were all methods I didn't approve.

"It's fine. What Rodrigo gave me is enough, I don't need any more mines or mansions or greenhouses."

Their shoulders slumped.

"If we had known, we wouldn't have blown it up," Kalen mumbled quietly.

I immediately knew that he was talking about the glass greenhouse that they had destroyed.

"You never know what Rodrigo might give me. He's a very generous man."

I wasn't saying that to show off, but rather to imply that they shouldn't destroy anything that belonged to Rodrigo, since he might gift it to me. Kalen, Ada, and Ayla scowled. They didn't seem happy about this.

The imperial palace banquet was so extravagant that its

purpose seemed to be to flaunt the empire's power. The floor was lined with jewel-encrusted tiles, sparkling in the light of the chandeliers like galaxies. The palace musicians played serene music endlessly. The nobles who had already arrived had gathered in small groups and were busy chatting and sampling the food prepared by the imperial palace.

It was only when the Kartinas arrived that silence fell over the banquet hall. Everyone had their eyes fixed toward the doors. On a specific person, to be exact.

Me.

"W-wait, what am I looking at right now?"

"Stop drooling. She's dating Sir Rodrigo."

"She's a goddess!"

"That's an understatement."

The men were unable to lift their jaws back up from the floor.

"Maybe they'll stop gawking if I tear their jaws apart," Kalen muttered ominously.

"We should put bibs on them."

"Better yet, we should poke their eyes out."

Vicious comments came from Ayla and Ada on either side of me.

"Let's just go." Worried that my siblings would actually put their words into action, I hurriedly grasped the skirts of my dress and took a step forward. Just a single step was enough to make the men around us let out a simultaneous sigh.

It's so tiresome to be pretty. I grumbled to myself, looking around. *More importantly, where is Rodrigo?*

I searched for Rodrigo, scanning the banquet hall. I couldn't catch sight of him even though he always stood out. *He's probably running late.*

"Let's find a quiet corner."

We fell in step with Kalen.

"Estella."

When we reached the middle of the banquet hall, I heard a voice calling me from behind. The women standing in front of me blushed furiously. Their eyes were fixed past my shoulder.

Rodrigo must be here.

Unlike the silence that had fallen at my entrance, when Rodrigo made his appearance, it got noisier. I slowly turned around. There really was no other way to describe the man in front of me except that he was insanely handsome. Even the most unrealistically gorgeous actors from my previous life would look ugly next to him.

"Welcome, Rodrigo."

And this man was my lover. He would become my husband someday too. Just until the female lead showed up, though. My back straightened with pride. There was no better accessory than a handsome man, after all.

"May I escort her now?" Rodrigo glanced at Kalen, who quickly ducked out of the way.

Kalen had promised Estella that he would apologize, but he didn't want to do it right now. That was why he was avoiding Rodrigo, as if he hadn't noticed him. It was the same for Ayla and Ada. They slowly backed away from Estella, though they didn't stop glaring at Rodrigo.

"Hm, this seems like a pretty nice outcome, considering I only lost one greenhouse."

"Don't say that." I tried to discourage him, thinking he might give me another strange present. Rodrigo laughed. The pleasant sound of his laughter was like a fresh breeze. It felt as if peace had returned at last—but not for long.

"Lady Estella."

Ugh, not this damn fool.

I forced a smile and turned around. Crown Prince Detheus and his sister Delia were heading straight toward us. Detheus' snakelike eyes scanned me from top to bottom. It made my skin crawl.

Detheus held out a hand. He wanted me to take it, and he seemed determined to kiss the back of my hand after failing last time. There weren't many noble ladies who could refuse the crown prince, especially when everyone was watching.

I had no choice but to raise my hand. The crown prince looked at me expectantly. It was like I could see straight into his dark thoughts.

Ugh, I really don't want to. If I could pay to refuse him, I would pay a billion gold bars. I shuddered at the thought of Detheus' lips making contact with my hand.

Tap.

"What's this?" Detheus' voice trembled, laced with surprise and annoyance. Rodrigo had put his hand on Detheus'! I stared blankly at Rodrigo.

"It's my hand," Rodrigo said smoothly.

"I'm asking what you think you are doing."

"Ah, you see, it seemed like you wanted to kiss a hand, Your Highness. So why not mine?" Rodrigo smiled faintly, an incredibly cold smile, and the banquet hall erupted with whispers.

TWENTY-FIVE

"Ah, you see, it seemed like you wanted to kiss a hand, Your Highness. So why not mine?"

Detheus glared at Rodrigo, his eyes wide at the audacity. I could relate. What Rodrigo had just done was beyond wild.

"Do you not like men's hands?"

"Now see here, Sir Rodrigo. This has nothing to do with gender—"

"Is it written anywhere in noble etiquette that men can't have their hands kissed? That's not what I learned."

Rodrigo was right. Nowhere did it explicitly say that getting a kiss on the back of the hand was reserved exclusively for women. In fact, the hand-kiss had originally been invented to greet the emperor more formally.

If there was anything inappropriate about what Rodrigo was doing, it was only that he was lower in rank than him. However, Detheus couldn't tactfully point this out, and his expression turned into a grimace.

Pfft! In the end, I was unable to hold back a small laugh. Detheus' look of disgust was priceless.

"How rude, Lady Estella." Delia glared at me, making no attempt to hide her displeasure.

Hm? Me? I was baffled. Sure, laughing at the crown prince might have been rude, but Rodrigo had been rude first. *You should chide Rodrigo, not me. Being blinded by love is no excuse. More importantly, is she picking a fight with me?*

As a Kartina, there was no backing out of a challenge, but I had no intention of clashing with the princess when so many people were watching. Plus, it seemed like Rodrigo needed my help. I ignored Delia and turned back toward Rodrigo.

"That's right. Rodrigo, that was rude. You've been neglecting my hand for far too long." I tugged at Rodrigo's sleeve, his hand still on Detheus'. Rodrigo raised his eyebrows before his eyes crinkled into a smile. I could practically hear Detheus and Delia's facade crumble at the sight of Rodrigo's smile, which was warm enough to melt ice.

It would be best to get away while Detheus and Delia were unable to react out of sheer bewilderment. I linked arms with Rodrigo. "Enjoy your time, Your Imperial Highnesses."

We quickly moved away from Detheus and Delia. Once we were far enough away, Rodrigo snickered. It was a mischievous laugh.

"Do you find that funny? I was terrified," I said.

When Rodrigo placed his large hand on top of Detheus', I wasn't the only one who was caught by surprise. Detheus' personal guards, who knew his nasty temper far too well, had also tensed up. The banquet hall had nearly become a battlefield.

"There's music, so why don't we dance together properly this time?" Rodrigo effortlessly changed the topic as my expression darkened.

I didn't think twice and put my hand on Rodrigo's shoulder. I could see Detheus and Delia looking for a chance to talk to us. Surely, they wouldn't try and talk to us on the dance floor. *I hope this doesn't mean we'll have to dance through the whole banquet.*

"Sure." Rodrigo gave a small nod.

Maybe it was because we had danced together before, but it was much easier for us to fall into step this time. The music wasn't too fast. It was the perfect tempo to have a conversation.

"I have a question."

"Ask anything you like."

"You don't like men, do you?"

Rodrigo scowled, replying, "No."

Is he gritting his teeth? "I know. I was just making sure."

As if a violent, R-rated novel aimed at male readers would ever have a gay male lead. It was definitely not a plot point that suited such stories.

Rodrigo was definitely straight. I had only doubted him for a moment because he had uncharacteristically demanded a kiss on his hand from the crown prince. *I'm glad he's not gay. Now I just have to find the female lead so he can be at peace, and then I'll be off to an island with the Kartinas.*

"What are you thinking about?" Rodrigo asked.

"Nothing."

"I can tell you're lying," he said.

"Does magic let you see things like that too?"

"Of course," Rodrigo took me by the waist and spun me around effortlessly. He continued, after making sure I found my footing again, "not."

I had been expectantly listening for more and couldn't hide my disappointment. *It would be so nice. A magic lie detector.*

Eventually, I said, "I wasn't thinking about anything."

I lied once more, knowing that he couldn't tell for sure.

"It's written all over your face," he said.

"Can you read my thoughts just by looking at my face?"

"Yes."

What an amazing skill.

Rodrigo and I danced two steps to the left. The sight of everyone moving in unison was like a dream, like something straight out of a movie, and it gave me a little thrill. Or maybe it was because I was dancing so much.

"Then go ahead and tell me what I was thinking about."

Rodrigo smiled, a careful, charming smile. He said, "About how to run away."

Shock washed over me like cold water. Rodrigo was almost spot on. From his point of view, my plan to hand him off to the female lead and leave to go live on an island could sound like I was trying to run away.

How uncanny.

"You're wrong." I wasn't lying either, seeing that it was more accurate to say that I was trying to fulfill my end of the bargain rather than running away. Rodrigo seemed like he had something to say, but then the song was over.

"Let's go get something to drink," I suggested. My cheeks felt hot, and I wanted to drink something cold. Rodrigo offered his arm to me, and I placed my hand on it.

I hadn't officially declared him as my partner for the evening, but Rodrigo slid into the role of escorting me. Just then, a few palace maids passed by us carrying trays of cold drinks. Rodrigo took two glasses from the trays and handed me one. He immediately lifted his glass to his lips.

"Wait!" I cried out.

Rodrigo looked down at me, the glass still at his lips. I exchanged my glass for his, which made him frown.

"You have more enemies than I do," I told him.

I had seen it in the story. There had been a scene where someone poisoned Rodrigo's drink. Of course, it most likely wasn't something that would happen today. The tray had too many glasses, and there were too many people around.

There was no way the glass Rodrigo had happened to choose was the one that was poisoned, but I still wanted to swap with him because I didn't like the idea of him being in danger. If something happened to him, the first suspects would be the Kartinas.

"Am I the only one in danger?"

The Kartinas have a lot of enemies as well.

"It's fine as long as you're safe."

He pressed his lips together when I muttered this.

"If you suspect something," he said, "we should both avoid the drinks." Rodrigo took my glass and placed it on a table.

But I'm thirsty. And I can handle a bit of poison. I swapped glasses with him so confidently because I had built up a tolerance to most poisons.

"Next time, I should prepare drinks for us beforehand."

"That's not a bad idea."

How unfortunate that we don't have any with us today.

Rodrigo and I leaned against the wall, watching people mingling in the banquet hall. Judging by the merry laughter, they were enjoying the event. At times, I could sense people shooting glances at us. Some of them talked about us. There were comments that praised us, saying that we looked pretty and handsome, and others that criticized us, saying that we looked arrogant.

I ignored them all and kept my gaze straight ahead. None of them knew that I could hear them anyway, so there was no use getting offended.

"Come to think of it, where is His Majesty the Emperor?"

When I mentioned the emperor, Rodrigo's face darkened noticeably. "He will be here. He likes being the center of attention."

Rodrigo was nice enough to explain that the emperor was being fashionably late. He was acting and speaking gently, but as soon as I mentioned the emperor, a wall seemed to have gone up around Rodrigo. I sensed a sudden distance between us.

"Isn't His Holiness the Pope attending today as well? I'm curious to see what he's like." I began to bring up whatever came to mind, feeling awkward because of Rodrigo's change in attitude. Rodrigo responded with uncharacteristically short answers. It was mostly things like "I'm not sure," and "We shall find out soon."

"There he is."

Just as I had been growing tired of his short responses, Rodrigo nodded toward the doors. A fanfare rang out and magic fireworks erupted. Three people entered through the large doors. Emperor Thereo, Pope Nathaniel, and—

"Mom?"

Hela Kartina alongside them.

SIDE STORY

Emperor Thereo and Pope Nathaniel showing up together was one thing, but it was unusual for Hela to enter the banquet hall with them. Rodrigo seemed to be thinking the same.

"I have a bad feeling about this," he said, and I squeezed his arm harder.

When he looked down at me, I said, "I was thinking the same thing."

Rodrigo let out a huff of laughter and patted the back of my hand. My heart ached to see that the thought of misfortune made him laugh.

"Ah, don't frown, Estella," he said, with an odd expression. "Hunches like this are usually wrong."

I wanted to believe him. He started to move his hands toward my face, but soon paused.

"May I touch you, just for a moment?" Rodrigo asked, pointing at my face. "I thought I might use some magic."

"What kind of magic?" It was a habit of mine to be suspicious.

"A spell that makes you feel better, like nothing bad will happen."

Hm. I knew he had the potential to become a great mage and would become the greatest mage on the continent in the future, but this was hard to believe.

Rodrigo let out another huff of laughter at my skeptical look. "I won't do it if you don't want me to."

It must have been some sort of reverse psychology, because as soon as he lowered his hand, I got impatient. I snapped, "Do it!"

"All right, excuse me then." He used his two thumbs to press down on the corners of my mouth and lift them up. "You just smile like this."

Huh? What? I gave him a strange look with a smile that didn't reach my furrowed eyebrows, and he laughed once again.

"I find that it helps when you force a smile." He lowered his hands.

Hela, who had been walking behind Thereo and Nathaniel until they reached the middle of the banquet hall, turned on her heels and headed straight toward me. Rodrigo straightened up and faced her. I had never seen such a frigid expression on Hela's face.

My heart throbbed unpleasantly. I remembered what Rodrigo had said and forced a smile. As I lifted the corners of my lips, I could almost still feel his thumbs there. It made me feel better.

While Hela made her way toward us, Thereo and Nathaniel ignored all the nobles greeting them and haughtily stalked up to their respective thrones. Although the pope's throne sat a step lower than the emperor's, both thrones bore a striking resemblance.

The pope's authority is truly impressive.

Hela came to a stop in front of me, and Rodrigo took half a step to the side so Hela and I could greet each other.

"Estella, you are my bluebird as always." Bluebirds were a symbol of joy. Hela pressed a couple of light kisses on each of my cheeks.

"Greetings, Duchess Hela. May the grace of God be with you." As our greeting started to drag out, Rodrigo chimed in at an appropriate time.

Hela fixed her icy-cold gaze on him. Her voice was steel as she said, "It's been a while, Sir Rodrigo."

But Hela greeted him, always elegant and full of grace. *Mom is greeting Rodrigo?* I had been worried that Hela might simply ignore him, but I was glad and thankful that she greeted him.

"If you have time, could I have a word with you, Your Grace?" Hela asked Rodrigo.

CHAPTER
TWENTY-SIX

"If you have time, could I have a word with you, Your Grace?" Hela asked Rodrigo.

I blinked for a moment before coming to my senses. "P-pardon?"

My thoughts muddled in my head. She might not have made it obvious, but the person who was most firmly against my relationship with Rodrigo was Hela. They say the burning coal's hotter than the fire, and quiet anger was scarier than screaming.

I had been on edge. Hela might get rid of Rodrigo one day using a method no one would have ever thought of—but now she was greeting him and wanting to talk to him.

"Estella, would you let me borrow your... lover for a moment?" She had paused in between, but she even used the word "lover."

"Of course, mom." I took Hela's hand, and she turned to look at me.

Thank you, mom. I mouthed to her. Hela's brows furrowed slightly.

Wait... is this a trap? But it was too late to take back my words now.

"Since we have her permission, let's find somewhere to talk, Your Grace."

"Will you be all right on your own, Estella?" Rodrigo's tone dripped with sweetness, like honey, maybe because Hela was there.

I could feel my nose tingling, so I quickly ran my hand over it and pushed him forward. "You don't need to worry about me."

"I'm afraid your beauty might attract flies."

"That won't happen," I replied.

Rodrigo hummed skeptically as if he didn't believe me, but there really was no chance for any man to even get close to me—as soon as Rodrigo left, Kalen, Ada, and Ayla approached me.

"Let's dance!" Kalen held his hand out to me.

"It would be my honor, Kalen."

"I'm next."

"No, I'm next!" Ayla and Ada bickered over who would dance with me next.

"You can't. Women are supposed to dance with men," Kalen muttered, putting a stop to Ayla and Ada's argument.

"Says who? Didn't you see Rodrigo earlier? Putting his hand on top of the crown prince's? Is it written anywhere that women can only dance with men? Hm?" Ayla growled as she stepped up to Kalen, almost reaching up to his jaw.

"That's right, Kalen. I'll dance with you, Ayla, and Ada as well. We all danced together when we practiced as children." I jumped in to mediate. I didn't want the imperial banquet to be ruined. Kalen had no choice but to back off because the next song had started.

"I can't miss out on even a second of dancing with you!" Kalen took my hand.

Sadly, the song was over all too soon. Next was Ayla, and I danced to the third song with Ada. Everyone stared in awe at the peculiar sight of sisters dancing together.

"Where are we going?" Rodrigo came to a halt after silently following Hela's lead for a while.

Hela was leading him straight toward the emperor's table.

"You've been summoned by the emperor."

Damn. Rodrigo clenched and unclenched his fists. He was uncomfortable facing Thereo because he knew what the emperor wanted from him.

Thereo wanted to keep Rodrigo under his thumb. An Erhart who moved and acted on the emperor's whim like a puppet. Rodrigo and his parents had refused to play the part.

It was then that Thereo's bullying worsened. It wasn't simply the emperor keeping Rodrigo in check—it was unmistakable bullying, and Rodrigo had avoided the emperor since then. If he was called to the imperial palace for no particular reason, Rodrigo always refused, using his work or health as an excuse.

But Thereo refused to leave Rodrigo alone. Whenever Rodrigo declined an invitation, an assassin would break in and problems would arise in Rodrigo's business endeavors. Despite all this, Rodrigo couldn't face Thereo.

"Rodrigo, you must... survive."

"Bright places can be... the best place to go unnoticed. Don't hide..."

A horrible memory flashed through Rodrigo's mind. The deaths of the previous Archduke and Archduchess Erhart had been sudden. Rodrigo suspected Thereo, but his parents, even with their dying breaths, had insisted that he not suspect anyone and simply survive. They worried about Rodrigo until the very end.

They had not been able to close their eyes in peace. In the end, it was Rodrigo who had to close their eyes.

"You can still turn back. However, know that this will be your only chance to get approval for your relationship with Estella, Your Grace."

Rodrigo paused. *In other words, according to Hela, if I meet with the emperor now, I can date Estella without the Kartinas' disapproval?*

It would be advantageous if the Kartinas stopped messing with the Erhart business. And it would be good for him as well.

Rodrigo answered without thinking twice. "Let us go."

On the day of the banquet, Nathaniel had been in a bad mood all day. Mostly because of the message he had received from an informant assigned to spy on Erhart.

"Red dragon, blue dragon, genuine."

It meant that the relationship between Estella Kartina and Rodrigo Erhart seemed genuine. Nathaniel crumpled up the paper. Infused with magic, the paper disintegrated into dust and disappeared in his hand.

If the Kartinas and the Erharts started getting along, it would be bad for Nathaniel in many ways. For starters, if the two houses became more powerful and the aristocracy united because of them getting along, the throne would lose power. In turn, the papal court, which was supported by the throne, would lose power as well.

"And war wouldn't be easy, either."

The empire was strong, but small conflicts still broke out frequently along the border regions, simply because the empire was still politically unstable.

The papal court publicly discouraged war, but secretly they sold weapons and seized both honor and riches. In this way, the enmity between the Kartinas and the Erharts had a great influence on the entire continent.

On the empire, its neighboring nations, and the papal court.

Nathaniel, who had been controlling the situation and using Thereo like a chess piece from the shadows, now had no choice but to make a move himself. It looked as though his golden goose was about to die, and he would be neglecting his duties if he didn't step up.

Nathaniel met up with Thereo, and together they designed a satisfying solution—after which they called the Kartinas. This was why Nathaniel, Thereo, and Hela had shown up at the banquet together.

Thereo smiled smugly at the sight of Rodrigo bowing deeply toward him.

"You must be doing well, you look good."

It was all thanks to Estella. Rodrigo had been able to rid himself of years' worth of exhaustion just by the few hours of deep sleep he had gotten while she sat by him. Rodrigo recalled that restful sleep and waited for the day he would be able to sleep that deeply once more.

And for that to happen, I'll have to overcome this obstacle first.

Rodrigo's gaze shifted from Hela to Thereo, and then to Pope Nathaniel.

"May God's grace be with you. I am Nathaniel, God's servant," he said. "It is my honor to meet the empire's only archduke, Sir Rodrigo."

A *wily tongue*, Rodrigo concluded as he watched Nathaniel's mouth move and heard his soft voice.

"Good to meet you, Your Holiness," he replied curtly.

The pope held out his hand first. He was owed the same kind of formality as the emperor. Although the pope was allowing the emperor to be in a higher position for the time being, the pope would occasionally be on top. Just as with Thereo and Nathaniel.

For that reason, the pope bowed to no one. There were two empires on the continent, and both emperors were under Nathaniel's thumb.

The greatest sign of hospitality that the pope could give was to offer a handshake. Nathaniel was offering Rodrigo the highest greeting he could give, but Rodrigo simply stared at the emperor's hand without taking it.

"Haha, is there something on my hand?" Nathaniel laughed lightly.

"No, but..." Rodrigo trailed off, even though he had something to say. Then he took Nathaniel's hand, hesitating because he had noticed a faint green light emanating from it. What was it? He had a bad feeling.

Just as expected, as soon as Rodrigo took his hand, lightning shot through his body. At the unpleasant feeling, Rodrigo concentrated on his hand. Their handshake lasted for a while. Hela sensed the strange tension between them and cleared her throat.

"You've got quite the strength, Your Grace."

Nathaniel let go first. Rodrigo glared at him.

"His Majesty is waiting, so why don't we all have a seat?" Hela said in an attempt to lighten the mood.

At Hela's words, Nathaniel and Rodrigo finally sat down. Thereo waved away the people around them to examine the food laid out on the table for the four of them. Thereo was the first to lazily pick up his teacup.

"The Kartinas are a nice sight to behold." Thereo's gaze was directed toward the dance floor, where Estella and Ada were dancing together.

Rodrigo turned to watch Estella as well. She was smiling brightly, as if she was genuinely enjoying herself. Her smile was radiant enough to lift his mood, too. People around them stood there, staring as if confused by the sight of two women dancing together.

Are they speaking ill of them? Rodrigo tensed. But contrary to his worry, everyone soon began to smile. The skirts of the two women's dresses fluttered like butterfly wings whenever they spun around, and their bright laughter was angelic. Their joy seemed to spread to everyone watching.

Rodrigo's heart warmed as well. If the emperor hadn't begun talking to him, Rodrigo would have been happy for a good long while.

"Rodrigo, I hear you're dating someone. I thought it was a lie, but I see that it's true." Thereo said, catching sight of the smile on Rodrigo's lips.

Rodrigo quickly schooled his expression. He asked, "What reason would I have to lie about my relationship?"

"Yes, you're right. Haha, how nice. I was worried since you rejected all the women I introduced you to."

An unbelievably low-brow joke came out of the emperor's mouth. Hela could tell that the woman the emperor was referring to was Delia. Hela looked away as she sipped her tea.

"The princess was very disappointed."

Hela paused, her teacup at her lips, at Delia being mentioned. She glanced at Rodrigo, able to tell by the way his brows furrowed ever so slightly that he had absolutely no interest in Delia. Rodrigo didn't reply.

He was barely listening to Thereo because he was busy keeping an eye on Nathaniel, who sat across from him. Nathaniel was an unpleasant man. His eyes, hiding behind a crescent smile, were menacing. It was extremely unpleasant to see those menacing eyes darting back and forth between him and Estella.

"Is there something you wish to tell me, Your Majesty?" Rodrigo, who wanted to leave, urged Thereo to continue.

"Ah, I almost forgot. It's been so long since I've seen you, so small talk takes a while. Come by the imperial palace more often. Once you're done wrapping up this war, that is."

War? Rodrigo, who had been reaching for his teacup, paused.

"It's time to do your duty as the archduke. Go and conquer the Veloki Peninsula."

"What do you mean by war? Did I hear that correctly?" Rodrigo was indirectly refusing his order. But Thereo was determined and didn't intend to back off.

Expressing his strong will to drive Rodrigo to the warfront, he continued. "You jest. I've already informed the imperial troops that you will be joining them. Everything is ready, so just pack lightly and be on your way. Why don't you leave tomorrow morning?"

"That was so much fun, Estella! How about another one?" asked Ada, who'd been the last to dance with me.

"I need some water."

Kalen, Ayla, and Ada had only danced to one song each, but I had danced along to three songs in a row. If you counted the dance with Rodrigo, I'd already danced four times. It wasn't that I was tired, but I was starting to sweat. And since I would see Rodrigo again, I didn't want to smell sweaty.

Ada seemed disappointed, but didn't complain and quickly fetched a glass, trying it first before handing it to me. I glanced over at Rodrigo as I leaned against the wall, sandwiched between Ada and Ayla.

Rodrigo loathed Thereo. Near the end of the novel, Rodrigo got his revenge. They discovered Thereo's corpse, devoid of blood and innards, in a room Rodrigo had come out of. It was horrific, but it was evidence of how much Rodrigo despised the emperor.

The fact that he was able to calmly talk to the person he hated so much was quite remarkable.

"Poor Kalen."

At Ayla's mumbled comment, my eyes began searching for my brother. Kalen, who had been with us just a moment ago, was now surrounded by elderly nobles.

"Because dad's not here."

Because you two abandoned the western border. If Ada and Ayla had any sort of conscience, they would have felt guilty, but they seemed completely unbothered. The two of them laughed loudly while they drank their wine.

"Father is taking too long, don't you think?" I pointed out. I expected Stefan to take care of the situation very quickly, but he still hadn't returned, days after he was supposed to be back.

"Are you worried about him?" Ada asked, surprised.

"He wouldn't even break a sweat if all of us attacked him at once. He'd defeat us with no problem since he has so much experience."

I nodded at Ayla's words. Stefan was, in many ways, an amazing man. The speed at which he operated and the way he wrapped everything up without any loose ends, he really was a model villain.

"It's just that he's taking so long." But I couldn't help worrying. In the novel, the villains' lives ended horrifically. With me trying to change the outcome of the story, Stefan's life might also have deviated from the plot.

"I guess the monsters were stronger than usual, right?"

Ayla and Ada began describing the monsters they had seen in the western borderlands. I had little interest in monsters. Even in the novel, monsters were only mentioned briefly.

It was clear that the author hadn't been very interested in monsters, either. Everything else had been described with exhaustive detail, but the monsters...

[*The Kartinas went to the western border to take care of the monsters.*]

[*Stefan destroyed a village on his way home from killing monsters.*]

[*The Kartinas met up at the monster hunting grounds.*]

That was all. Descriptions about what the monsters were exactly, or what types there were, were mostly left out. In retrospect, it wasn't a very well-written novel. Having lived in the novel for a while now, I was able to tell just how much detail had been left out.

It was very protagonist-centric.

Everything revolved around the main character. Maybe that was why my eyes kept drifting toward Rodrigo. His expression of forced calm was slowly giving way to annoyance.

I think I should rescue Rodrigo. I looked around the banquet hall, searching for an excuse to approach the emperor's table. At that moment, I saw Detheus heading toward me.

Bingo!

CHAPTER
TWENTY-EIGHT

"I was really looking forward to what you would be wearing, since you sent back the dress I designed for you. As expected, you do not disappoint, Lady Estella."

I hate the way this guy looks at me, but the way he speaks is even worse. What a gross way to say that he's still mad at me for refusing his gift. I took a slow, deep breath to keep my cool. This must be the first time a compliment has put me in a bad mood.

I put on a smile and curtsied, greeting him before he could hold out his hand again. Detheus held a glass of alcohol, and judging by his smell, he had already consumed quite a few glasses. It seemed like Detheus was the only one enjoying the banquet without a care.

"I'll take that as a compliment."

"It is. It's my praise for your ever so blinding beauty." Detheus sneakily dropped the formalities. It completely ruined my mood.

"Your Highness, they say the alcohol these days is quite strong."

Stop acting like a drunkard and snap out of it. I couldn't bring myself to tell him to get lost. After all, I had to use him to get closer to the emperor's table. *So snap out of it already. If you keep acting like some sort of backstreet thug, it really makes me want to kill you, you know.*

"Oh, sorry. I felt comfortable because we've seen each other often," he said. "Anyway, would you like to dance? The music is quite pleasant."

"I've already danced four times, so I'm a bit tired." I refused, pretending like it was a shame that I had to.

"Haha, I saw you dancing with Lady Ayla and Lady Ada. You must be close with your sisters."

"Yes, I'm very fortunate. My siblings cherish me so much that they keep saying they'll eradicate whoever even looks at me from the face of the continent." Technically, my siblings had said they'd poke their eyes out, but I toned it down. Somehow, it sounded even more violent.

Detheus let out a laugh. "You are just like a hedgehog." Detheus gestured toward the balcony with his glass. "If you won't dance with me, how about a little talk somewhere quiet?"

Does he not know what that implies? The drinks must have gone straight to his head. It's like his brain is completely submerged in alcohol. What a thoughtless man.

I took a step back. It was a roundabout way of refusing his offer.

"I would like to meet His Holiness the Pope, though. Could you introduce me to him?" I suggested instead.

Detheus' mouth stretched into a frown. My string of refusals must have upset him. He probably couldn't understand why I was refusing him when he was the handsome, rich, and powerful crown prince. *All those other women would just fall for you immediately when you offered them things like jewels and dresses, or even mansions and titles, right?*

The fact that he thought that way made it clear that Detheus' character was rotten to the core.

"His Holiness is not very friendly. You might just be ignored, Lady Estella."

"It's just a greeting, there isn't much to ignore." I smiled.

Detheus' expression wavered, and he let out a deep sigh. Then he downed the contents of his glass in one go and replied, "All right, I'll introduce you."

Detheus held out his hand, offering to escort me, but I quickly grasped the skirts of my dress with both hands.

"My dress is so long," I said, "it's hard to walk. I don't know why they make them so long these days." *I have no intention of holding your hand.*

Detheus frowned as if he was displeased, but then he laughed. "You are one charming woman."

But you looked really mad a second ago.

Detheus walked past me, and I quietly followed him. On our way, a few people who approached to talk to Detheus backed off after they saw his sour expression.

"Has the Veloki Peninsula not been friendly with the empire for generations?"

The Veloki Peninsula. This angular, stick-shaped peninsula stuck out of the northwestern end of the empire, which was more of a round shape overall. Surrounded by the ocean on three sides, it was rich in seafood, had a large navy, and was overall a pleasant place to live.

It was no exaggeration to say that the Veloki Peninsula was at the center of the growing trade industry because it had maximized its locational strengths. There was a saying that there were so many rich people on the Veloki Peninsula that even the beggars there ate steaks. Thanks to its robust navy, the strongest on the continent, as well as its ideal location, it was relatively safe from foreign invasion. The only nation close to it was the empire, and the Veloki Peninsula had never been aggressive toward them.

It was smart of them, really.

The Veloki Peninsula had never once been late in paying taxes to the empire. Whenever the empire raised taxes, they paid them without complaint. They never sent envoys to negotiate, like other countries did. And whenever they got hold of the highest quality products, they offered some to the emperor first.

In other words, they were like loyal dogs to the empire. Because of this, the two nations have never clashed, so why now?

"It seems that the young king is hostile."

Ah. Rodrigo recalled the young man who had been crowned king recently. He had met him once, when Rodrigo had gone to the Veloki Peninsula because of a permit issue regarding a distribution business he was operating there.

He was a prince back then, but I guess he's the king now. The man had left a lasting impression. Eyes burning with ambition, and a calm facade in contrast.

"Has there been any direct harm to the empire?"

"No, no," Thereo explained. "Rodrigo, you're still so young. Just because they haven't raised their swords against the empire yet doesn't mean there aren't any other problems."

Thereo went on to explain that their power must be contained. Just as a wound festers when it is left untreated, the peninsula could one day become a great danger to the empire.

"Is it really necessary to strike first—"

"I apologize for interrupting your conversation. It has been a while since I last saw His Holiness, so I wanted to greet him."

Rodrigo was in the middle of trying to persuade Thereo when Detheus arrived. Thereo was glad he was here. He was obviously becoming annoyed by Rodrigo's stubborn insistence on arguing, but now he could change the subject. The command had been given, so Rodrigo would have no choice but to leave for the warfront.

"May the holy kiss of God be with you. It's good to see you looking so happy, Your Highness."

"May we join you? This is—"

"My lover."

"My daughter."

Rodrigo and Hela spoke up at the same time as Detheus tried to introduce her. Neither of them could stand the sight of Detheus acting as if he had anything to do with Estella. Hela and Rodrigo turned to glance at each other, then immediately looked away. Estella had a moment to introduce herself.

"Good evening. As you just heard, I am Estella, the youngest daughter of the Kartinas as well as Sir Rodrigo's lover."

Nathaniel's gaze lingered on Estella as she placed a hand on her chest and curtsied.

"On my way in, I heard people compare your beauty to that of a goddess. I believed them to be insolent comments at first, but..." Nathaniel stood from his throne and took two steps down to where Estella stood. She caught sight of his pristine white shoes.

How can someone's shoes be that spotless? It would be perfect for a bleach commercial, Estella mused as she raised her head. She met Nathaniel's golden eyes and watched as his lips spread slowly into a smile.

"Their praise seems to have been insufficient." He said and held out his hand to Estella. "Will you refuse my greeting as well?"

A demand for her to place her hand on his. Estella's gaze wavered.

It was hard to gauge Nathaniel's intentions. *I thought clergymen hated physical contact with outsiders.* He was smiling, but it wasn't a warm smile. His gaze was cold, piercing through me.

I don't want to take his hand. I began to pout, but quickly stopped myself. Then I lightly placed my hand on top of his palm. Nathaniel smiled and Rodrigo's expression hardened.

"May God's grace be with you." Instead of a kiss, Nathaniel stroked the back of my hand with his thumb, gave me a blessing, and let go.

"Good to see you. Take a seat," said Emperor Thereo.

I sat down next to Rodrigo, and he reached to hold my hand under the table.

What are you doing? I turned to look at him, but he didn't look at me. With a solemn expression, his eyes were fixed on Nathaniel.

"Let us continue our conversation. You must go to the Veloki Peninsula."

The Veloki Peninsula? What?

When I squeezed Rodrigo's hand, he glanced at me for a moment. "Later," he mouthed.

Does that mean he'll explain later?

But I couldn't help my curiosity. Because Emperor Thereo had addressed Rodrigo directly.

"Do you agree with this, Your Holiness? Isn't the papal court all about keeping peace? Do you believe this war to be necessary?" Rodrigo began interrogating Nathaniel.

I was starting to get impatient. *What in the world are they talking about? It sounds like they're talking about war. But on the Veloki Peninsula? Did the empire ever go to war with them?*

I quickly searched my memories. But I couldn't find an answer. I barely remembered anything about the Veloki Peninsula. *Damn it. I should have written down everything I remembered as soon as I was reborn.* I had placed too much faith in myself.

"Your Grace, the papal court can only pray for the good of the many."

"Do you believe that the few should be sacrificed for the many?"

Nathaniel made the sign of the cross. He closed his eyes for a moment and then smiled as he opened them again. It was a wicked, snake-like smile. He said, "All the papal court can do is pray for their souls to rest in peace."

Rodrigo clenched his hands into fists. It was the angriest I had ever seen him.

"Then it's decided. You must have a lot to prepare, so be on your way."

It was a command for him to leave. Rodrigo stood, nodded a quick bow, and turned on his heel. I glanced back and forth between Rodrigo, who was getting farther away, and Nathaniel, who was standing in front of me, before I too stood up.

"Please excuse me, I'm not feeling well."

Hela, who I was sure would stop me, waved her hand at me, telling me to go ahead. I hurried over to Rodrigo, almost breaking into a run.

"Rodrigo, Rodrigo!"

He was very quick on his feet. He had already exited the banquet hall and was now walking across the gardens. At the sound of my voice, he turned around. His eyes widened a bit, as if he hadn't expected me to follow him.

"Estella?"

"Why are you walking so fast?" I panted.

"I didn't expect you to follow," he said.

"Did you expect me to sit there and chat with the emperor, the crown prince, and the pope, all of whom you hate?"

His lips spread into a smile, as if he was moved by my words.

"What's got you so happy?" I asked.

"You following me. You not spending time with the people I hate."

"You really hate them, don't you?" *Understandably. But what was Nathaniel's role in the story? I thought I would remember if I met him, but I still have no idea.* "Are you going home?"

"Yes, I am. And I'll be leaving for the Veloki Peninsula tomorrow."

"I need an explanation."

"Will you walk with me?" said Rodrigo.

TWENTY-NINE

As an answer, I took the lead and started walking. The night air was chilly, helping me cool down after chasing Rodrigo. Behind me, Rodrigo let out a laugh. I liked the sound of his sudden laughter. I slowed down to walk next to him.

We moved along a winding, labyrinthian path and arrived at a wide-open garden. There was a fountain spouting water in the middle, with benches around it. That was our destination, and I quite liked the feeling of walking past dense groupings of trees. I also liked how quiet it was compared to the banquet hall.

"Ah!" Except for the fact that it was a little dark, so I couldn't see where I was going.

As I began to fall, Rodrigo stuck out his hand and caught me around the torso. His large biceps were firm as he helped steady me. His eyes shone in the moonlight. No artist could accurately portray Rodrigo's blood-red eyes. It was a color unique to Rodrigo. I felt like I could get lost in those eyes as I stared into them.

"I am going to war," he said, standing close to me.

"You don't have a choice?" I knew that it had already been decided, but I asked him anyway.

"That seems to be the case."

"Do you want to go?"

He smiled faintly. "I have never done anything I wanted to."

Oh... I shifted my gaze, unable to think of what to say. My heart ached at the resignation evident in his voice. For the first time, I felt like murdering the author.

How could you make his life so miserable? I know a happy ending is much more cathartic after a lot of strife, but this is too much.

I placed my hand on his cheek, and he flinched. I then asked slowly, "Is there anything you want to do right now?"

"And if there was?" Rodrigo's gaze wavered before returning to me.

"I'll let you do it." I spoke with confidence, as if I had become Cinderella's fairy godmother. I didn't have a magic wand or magical powers, but for whatever reason, I was sure that I would be able to grant whatever wish he had at this moment.

"Out of pity? I don't like being pitied."

"Me? Pity you? Come on, Rodrigo. You are the empire's archduke. You're a man who's got money, abilities, status, and power."

Technically, I did pity him. But objectively speaking, he really was someone who had everything.

"And?"

He demanded more. I wasn't sure why he needed me to inflate his ego, but he was acting like a child asking for praise, which was cute.

"And you're handsome. Anyone would be happy to be born with looks like yours."

Rodrigo smiled brightly.

"Not to mention your body. It's all strong and taut and—" I stopped mid-sentence. My hand had somehow made it up to his chest. I could feel his heart thumping under my palm. I looked up at him, my eyes wide in surprise. The smile on his face had vanished.

"I would like to kiss you."

Thump. My heart sank. I felt lightheaded for a moment as my heart seemed to drop into a bottomless pit.

"Do you not want me to?" He steadied me with his strong arms as I staggered.

I missed his playful smile. It wasn't that I didn't want to. But I did feel a bit guilty. Rodrigo belonged to the female lead. It weirdly felt like I was having an affair with him.

"If you don't want me to, I won't."

Apparently, he took my hesitation as a rejection because he let go of me and stepped away. Out of reflex, I held onto him. He did not resist as I pulled him closer. With my face buried in his chest, I continued, "I just need some time."

Thump, thump, thump. Is it his heart or mine?

"How long do you need? Waiting is hard."

I admit it had I have feelings for him. And I knew I would have to leave him someday. *The moonlight is nice. The breeze is cool and the scent of flowers in the wind is pleasant as well. It's just me and him right now, and only the earth, the sky, and the trees would know that we kissed here.*

So, wouldn't it be okay to indulge in my emotions just for a moment? I can think about the future later.

I closed my eyes and raised my head.

"Thank you," he whispered, his lips brushing against my forehead.

I was about to ask if that was all, but before I could speak, his lips pressed against mine. My lower lip tingled as he sucked on it and his tongue entered my mouth through the small gap. His breaths were short, coming out in hot bursts.

The kiss itself was incredibly slow and cautious. He kissed me as if I were made out of glass, which made me impatient. I wrapped my arms around his neck, and he shivered. His tongue explored my mouth as if it was mapping it out. My breath grew short at his insistent movement, as if committing this moment to memory.

Just as I grew so lightheaded that I thought I might faint, I pushed him away. He did not resist. The heated passion did not fade from his expression.

I hurriedly hid my face in my hands. I was overcome with belated embarrassment at kissing him so passionately. Rodrigo reached out and tucked me into his embrace.

Is he going to kiss me again?

To my disappointment, he simply held me. He patted my back as if he knew my heart was beating wildly and was trying to help calm it down. He asked, "When is your birthday?"

"May 10th."

"What a wonderful day to get married." His bright voice thickened. "I will make sure to be back by then."

It sounded just like a proposal. I was unable to reply with my face still buried in his chest. If war really broke out with the Veloki Peninsula, it wouldn't end so easily. I could only hope that he would make it back.

Just as Thereo had said, preparations had already been made. Rodrigo scowled as he watched the imperial troops that had gathered in front of his manor at dawn.

"You'll catch a cold." Augus handed him a towel.

Steam rose from Rodrigo's body as he stepped out of the bath. Rivulets of water ran between his taut muscles. Augus grew solemn at the sight of his master's radiant back. The scars all over his body were evidence of his arduous life.

There isn't even any room left on his body, but I'm sure he'll be getting another scar... It would be great if it was only one more scar. It could be two, or he could even lose his life this time.

Last night, Rodrigo called for an emergency meeting and told Devlon and Gunther to quit now if they planned on doing so—that the emperor had no intention of winning this war.

But he had told them that he had to win no matter what, and that it would be a harsh and difficult fight. Unsurprisingly, Gunther and Devlon had chosen to follow Rodrigo. Their faces had seemed somehow carefree as they had replied, in an annoyed tone, that none of their fights had ever been easy anyway.

But Augus wasn't feeling carefree. He didn't feel comfortable having to send them off. He placed a towel on

Rodrigo's shoulders from behind before stepping back. It was impossible to know what thoughts lay behind those red eyes.

"Augus."

"Yes, sir."

"Take good care of Estella for me."

"What do you mean?"

"Send her gifts whenever it seems appropriate. I made a list." Rodrigo gestured over to the desk. Augus' gaze traveled over to where he was pointing. He nodded after he spotted the list.

"Unless the Kartinas pose a great threat, don't fight them."

Augus committed this order to memory.

"If Estella visits the manor, treat her respectfully as if she's the archduchess."

Augus' eyes widened. "Are you really going to marry her?"

"If I come back." He set a condition.

Has he truly fallen in love?

"I'll also tell you what you want to know when I come back." Rodrigo was ready to face death.

Augus lowered his head. Tears rolled down his wrinkled face. A dark spot stained the carpet.

"Are you not going to see him off?" Jane asked me.

I had spent most of the night wide awake. I had been ill at ease ever since I had gotten back from the banquet. Jane, who knew it was because of Rodrigo being sent off to war, informed me that troops were moving to the Erhart manor and was adamant that I go and send him off.

But I couldn't go. I felt like this was all my fault. *No, it was my fault.*

Because there had been no mention of a war with the Veloki Peninsula in the novel. The pendulum of fate was swinging. Whenever he tried to get away from tragedy, fate dragged him back toward it.

Was it because I had approached him? I touched my forehead. The words he had said with his lips brushing against it echoed in my mind.

"Thank you."

I had no right to receive thanks from him.

"It's very uncharacteristic of you to think so much, my lady." Jane chided me. She brought out a dress and wrangled me into it after pulling off the clothes I had been wearing.

"Jane!"

"Go and send him off right now! Who knows when you'll ever see him again?" She pushed me forward.

"It's too late if I take a carriage now. We'll have to call the horseman, and—"

"You can go on horseback!"

Oh! Why didn't I think of that?

"I'll get a horse from the stables ready right away."

Jane threw open the doors. In front of us stood Kalen, Ada, and Ayla.

"K-Kalen?"

Damn it. They must be here to stop me.

"Come on, Estella. Let's go." He pulled me by the hand.

"What are you saying, Kalen?"

"You have to send him off. That's the right thing to do."

"A sendoff?"

"Weren't you going to see Sir Rodrigo?" Ada asked.

So... they're here because...

"We'll go with you. I'm better at riding than you. You can ride with me, Estella," said Kalen.

"We're not approving your relationship. We just thought someone going to war deserves at least a sendoff," Ayla quickly added, in case I misunderstood.

"Thank you."

I was truly thankful. Not because they were going with me, but because it felt like they were acknowledging Rodrigo, if only a little.

My heart swelled with joy.

"It is time to leave," Gunther said to Rodrigo, who couldn't help but continue to look back toward the end of the road.

Gunther knew who Rodrigo was waiting for.

Estella Kartina.

Ever since she had appeared, his master had changed. He considered it a good change. He was quite happy to see his master acting more like a normal human being instead of a machine. It was nice to see a real smile on a man who had always faked them. Devlon had been happy too, saying that their master was finally living a normal life. Gunther was grateful to Lady Estella.

But right now, he resented her. Gunther knew how dangerous it was to go into war with your thoughts divided.

"We should leave," Gunther urged once again.

Rodrigo turned to look at him.

"Let's go."

His voice was full of regret, but Gunther didn't hesitate to raise the banner. The sound of a horn rang out. The sun emerged from behind the clouds in time with the noise that served to wake everyone in the vicinity. The horses started to move at a slow yet steady pace.

CHAPTER THIRTY

"There they are!" Kalen cried out.

I peeked out from behind Kalen. Rodrigo's troops were marching in order. Kalen, Ada, and Ayla raced down the hill, and upon noticing them, a white flag was raised. The soldiers came to a halt. Rodrigo was at the head of the army. I jumped off even before Kalen's horse could stop.

"Estella!" Kalen shouted, panicked. His voice was full of worry for my safety, but thankfully, I wasn't injured. I ran straight to Rodrigo.

Rodrigo leaped from his horse and rushed toward me. I reached him without slowing down and jumped into his arms. He caught me and spun me around once before setting me down.

Someone let out a whistle. It was only then that I realized I had made it look like Rodrigo and I were passionate lovers, unable to live without each other. I felt a little embarrassed, knowing that hundreds of people were watching.

"I didn't get to say goodbye," I told him.

"A sendoff? What an honor."

"If you need help, write to me anytime."

Rodrigo nodded. But I knew he would never send such a letter.

"Don't forget that our deal includes marriage." I put my hands on his cheeks. He seemed a bit downtrodden, so I lightly tapped his cheeks to give him some energy. He smiled.

"I'm quite good at keeping promises. So don't worry, Estella."

That was how we parted.

Exactly one month after he left, war broke out. Rodrigo sent a request for more troops, but the emperor refused. That night, I packed my things.

"Where are you going, my lady?"

"I'm going to provide him with military support."

"What in the world are you talking about? Do you think going there on your own will solve anything?"

The war was not looking good. The troops provided by the emperor must have been a ragtag group, as they kept losing even small battles. Thankfully, Augus was in charge of tactical support, so they were at least well supplied.

"Jane, you're missing the bigger picture. I thought you had learned a lot by my side."

"Pardon?" Jane's eyes widened.

"I'm going to become a hostage."

"Wh-what do you mean?"

"I'm going to get captured by the Veloki. Who do you think will join the fight then?"

"The Kartinas, of course—"

"That's right, the Kartinas will join the fight."

Do not underestimate our military forces. Stefan even has an army of monsters. They're hard to control, but still. I felt bad for all the Veloki soldiers who would be massacred, but I had no other choice. Rodrigo is my priority.

"I'll be back, Jane."

"Let me go with you," she said.

"If we go together, they'll think we ran away from home."

"So, you're going to claim that people from Veloki came all the way here to kidnap you? You're the one not looking at the bigger picture, my lady."

"Do you have a better idea?"

Jane threw a few items of her own into a bag, saying, "You heard that your lover was in danger and left to go see him, and just before the reunion, Veloki bandits appeared... let's go with that story."

Jane, you're so smart. I nodded. I grabbed some paper, quickly writing a letter.

"Dear mom, dad, Kalen, Ada, and Ayla, I'm leaving to see Rodrigo. I'll be back safe, so don't worry too much."

Setting the pen down, finished letter in hand, I hesitated.

"What is it, my lady?"

"It'll be impossible for us to outrun the Kartina scouts, right?" I was suddenly faced with reality. The Kartina scouts consisted of the most elite horse riders. Their horseback riding skills were unrivaled. I wasn't a bad rider myself, of course, but there was no way I could outrun dozens of them taking turns riding at top speed to catch up to me.

"Let's take a portal." I looked at Jane.

"But then they'll know our destination right away."

Because a portal would leave a trace of where its last destination was.

"We'll split it up into five."

"Five?" she asked.

I picked up a few pillows and stacked them up. "We'll split our journey into five destinations. And our final one will be…"

I leaned toward Jane and whispered in her ear. Her eyes lit up.

"You're a genius, my lady."

Rodrigo met up with the King of the Veloki Kingdom. Franz, Royal Veloki.

"I never thought we would see each other again as enemies." Franz spoke formally to Rodrigo.

"I did not expect it either. I could not have imagined this would happen back when I helped you when you were still a prince."

Rodrigo and Franz knew each other well. When Franz had been shunned for being the son of a concubine, Rodrigo helped him out. He had been the key to Franz gaining a foothold in Veloki and finally being crowned king. To Franz, Rodrigo was a good friend and a benefactor.

"Are you really planning to fight us?" When Franz heard that the empire was sending an army, he was prepared to fight. He had organized his own army and evacuated the villages along the border. But as soon as he had found out that the empire's army was being led by Rodrigo, he hesitated. Instead of his army, Franz sent an envoy. That was how they had agreed to meet in a neutral zone.

"The empire is, yes."

"What I want to know is whether you, Sir Rodrigo, want to fight us. Veloki has been loyal to the empire all this time.

There is no reason for us to be attacked by them. This war has no justification. Even the empire can't justify it."

Everything Franz said was true, but Rodrigo couldn't be honest with him. Not because he didn't trust Franz, but because being honest wouldn't change anything.

"I am a mere servant of the empire."

"Come to our country." Franz' offer was exceptional. He offered Rodrigo a duchy and a position in the royal court. He offered him a territory to rule over and even the princess' hand in marriage, if he wished for it. The old Rodrigo would have gladly accepted this offer. But he had Estella now. He had promised to return by her birthday.

"I apologize."

Franz' face darkened at Rodrigo's polite refusal.

"If you must fight us, we will win," Franz shouted at Rodrigo, who got up to leave first.

"We won't lose, Your Highness." Rodrigo exited the tent with those last words. It wouldn't be an easy war. And it really wasn't. Rodrigo was unable to get any sleep because he spent the entire night strategizing.

The Veloki soldiers made up for what they lacked in experience with morale. Rodrigo's troops, on the other hand, excluding the Erhart soldiers, had lost all morale. And this difference was not something tactics could make up for.

A few small battles erupted. Unless the Erhart soldiers came into play, they lost every time. Soldiers began to flee one after another. Rodrigo took them out without hesitation.

Even as he heard himself being called a cold-blooded general, Rodrigo couldn't stop swinging his sword at the soldiers fleeing from battle. After all, letting even one of them go would encourage others to follow suit.

After slaying ten such deserters, Rodrigo got up from where he had laid down in the barracks and sat down at his desk. He hated the very idea, but he had to ask the emperor for reinforcements. If they received backup from the emperor, it would raise morale. It was worth a try.

Franz seemed to have no intention of an all-out-war. He knew how frightening Rodrigo was. *But once he finds out that the army is a complete mess...* It was only a matter of time until Rodrigo's forces would be overtaken. Rodrigo attached his message to the fastest falcon and sent it off.

A week later, the falcon returned. Rodrigo opened the letter.

"Request denied."

Those two words painfully wrenched at Rodrigo's heart. He had to think of another way, another plan.

"Gunther, Devlon," he called to them. Even lying in bed was a luxury he couldn't afford now.

The Kartina manor was in an uproar.

"The Lady has disappeared!" As the butler shouted, Stefan and Hela slowly emerged from their room.

And asked, "Which one?"

He could be referring to any one of their daughters, after all.

"It's Lady E-E-Estella..."

Stefan and Hela went deathly pale. Stefan began ringing the bell, and the manor's entire staff gathered out in the gardens.

"Estella has disappeared. What happened?" Stefan glared at the patrol guards first.

"We could not find any trace of her departure. There were no intruders last night, either."

"Are you saying that Estella just disappeared into thin air?" Stefan drew his sword and pointed it at the guards.

"Th-that's..."

"Father, we found it!" Just as Stefan's sword was about to pierce the neck of the patrol guard, Ayla came running up to them. Everyone turned to look at her.

"She took a portal!"

The Kartinas all hurried down into the basement, where the portals were set up. Five of the portals were emitting a dim light. Judging by the brightness of the light, it seemed as though it hadn't been more than three hours since the portals had been activated.

"Where did she go?" Stefan demanded of the mage in charge of portals.

At his frightening tone, the mage trembled and told him the five destinations. All five portals led to different places near the Veloki border. Hela staggered.

"Estella must have gone to see Rodrigo." Her voice was faint.

Stefan clenched his fists tightly. *That damn bastard! He's finally lured away my daughter! And to a dangerous warfront, at that!*

"Get moving immediately and find Estella!" Stefan's shout echoed through the basement.

"Are you all right, my lady?" Jane asked me.

I got to my feet, dusting off the grass stuck to the bottom of my skirt. I said, "I'm all right."

"That's incredible. I'm about to throw up."

Jane ended up leaning against a tree and throwing up. I held my nose and patted her back. There wasn't much in her stomach, so it didn't take long. *I guess it's true that people get motion sickness from portals.* But I had loved going on rides at amusement parks in my previous life, so the portals didn't affect me at all. My past life helped me out quite often.

"Hurry up and pull yourself together. The sun is rising."

Once the sun was up, they would know that I had disappeared, and we would start being chased. I had to meet Rodrigo, explain my plan, and volunteer to become a hostage to the Veloki Kingdom before they caught up to us. There was no time.

"Why didn't we teleport closer, then?" Jane grumbled as she wiped her mouth. "If I get on a horse right now, I'll die."

"Then let's get a carriage. I'll take the reins." I twisted my voluminous hair up into a bun and placed a cone hat over it. Dressed in men's clothing, I could pass as a young man. And Jane looked like a noble lady.

"Me, riding in a carriage driven by my lady...? What an honor," Jane replied.

This is why I liked Jane. The way she adjusted to every situation thrown at her made me think of a wily, adaptable little cat.

"Let's go find a carriage first."

Jane and I walked along the forest path.

"My lady, the only reason I am riding inside the carriage is to protect you. You know that, right? That a rich-looking young noble lady is an easy target?"

Yes, yes, I know. I nodded, listening to Jane's explanation that sounded more like an excuse. We were able to find a carriage to rent right away. Gold coins flowed out of Jane's pocket. I opened the carriage door for her, playing the part pretty well.

"By the way, do you even know how to drive a carriage, my lady?" Jane asked, with an uncertain look in her eyes, just as she was about to step inside.

To be continued...